MURDER.COM

MURDER.COM

A REUBEN FROST MYSTERY

HAUGHTON MURPHY

MYSTERIOUSPRESS.COM

OPEN ROAD

INTEGRATED MEDIA

NEW YORK

Cover design by Greg Mortimer

978-1-5040-3036-6

Published in 2016 by MysteriousPress.com/Open Road Integrated Media, Inc.
180 Maiden Lane
New York, NY 10038
www.mysteriouspress.com
www.openroadmedia.com

For my brothers, John and Joseph

MURDER.COM

One

"NOT ON YOUR LIFE!"

"We have to get off our aging backsides and see more people."

Reuben Frost, sitting at his desk at the law firm of Chase & Ward, sipped his morning coffee and recalled his wife Cynthia's admonition of the night before. The two of them had been eating dinner—alone—at their New York town house on East Seventieth Street when she remarked that they were spending too many evenings at home.

The reason for the Frosts' curtailment of their schedule had been that Cynthia had recently developed arthritis in her left ankle. Before that she had been vigorous and active, subject only to the minor annoyances and debilities that both she and her husband could expect in their seventies. But the arthritis was different. For the first time it had made her feel old. And, as a result, she untypically retreated from the busy New York social life she and her husband had always led during four decades of marriage. She had also begun doing more and more of her work as the long-standing director of arts grants at the Brigham Foundation at home, claiming that this was now possible thanks to her laptop.

Ever the understanding spouse, Reuben had gone along with

his wife's desire to slow things down, though he himself felt perfectly capable of coping with a full calendar. So he had been relieved the previous evening when she told him she had concluded that keeping on the go was the only realistic therapy for her and that they should try to resume a brisk schedule. It was the old Cynthia speaking, the dancer who in her performance days had always combated physical discomfort with increased activity.

Reuben himself had long since retired as an active partner of Chase & Ward LLP. Yet as one of the leaders who had seen the law firm grow and mature, he maintained a fatherly, or now perhaps grandfatherly, interest in its affairs. Recognized as one of the most distinguished firms in Manhattan, its lawyers—numbering five hundred at last count (five times the number when Reuben had begun work there)—served many Fortune 500 corporations, and had collective experience in advising clients in almost all fields of industry and finance. Reuben, who had served as the Executive Partner of the firm for several years, modestly did not take credit either for its expansion or sterling reputation, but his wife was aware that he was annoyed when others did.

Although the active practice of law was definitely behind him, Reuben dutifully went to the office every business day. Mostly those days were uncrowded, much to his distress, making him all the more eager for evening activities. Occasionally, though, one of his former colleagues would consult him on a problem, usually of a tricky ethical, rather than a legal, nature. But the knocks were infrequent on the door of his modest office, which contrasted with the grand space he had occupied as the Executive Partner at One Metropolitan Plaza with a view of New York harbor. His only regular visitor was his new, pert, and not very smart secretary, Terry Whalen, who he now shared with two other retired partners in equally modest quarters adjacent to his own. (Originally, these three retirees, along with two others who had since died, were known among the more irreverent associates as "the Five Little Peppers." That designation no longer applied, and as far as Reuben knew, the young smarties had not come up with a new nickname. Had they asked, he would have suggested "the Three Wise Men.")

Reuben was grateful that the firm had provided him with civilized, if plain, office space. He shuddered when he thought of the odious circumstances of a friend at a downtown rival who was one of several retired lawyers herded together in a common bull pen, referred to by that firm's jokesters (and not always kindly) as "the Nursing Home."

His coffee finished, Reuben decided that there was no time like the present to begin attempts to fill in the social calendar. He buzzed Ms. Whalen and asked her to track down Detective First Class Luis Bautista in the New York City Police Department, assigned to what was clumsily called Detective Borough Manhattan. While waiting, he recalled how Bautista and he had first met at the time of the murder of his partner, Graham Donovan. And how odd circumstances had brought them together in homicide investigations several times since.

Reuben and Cynthia had become close friends with Luis and his wife, Francesca. They had seen the young couple through their courtship and marriage and, more recently, through the birth of twins, Rafaela Cynthia and Manuel Reuben. The children's middle names had of course been taken from their honorary godparents—the Frosts—who, childless themselves, were delighted with the gesture.

"Thank heaven they're only two of them," Francesca had said

at the time, relieved that the fertility treatment she had undergone had not produced even more.

"How are the twins?" Reuben asked, once Bautista had been reached.

"Trouble and More Trouble, you mean? They're fine, Reuben. But two handfuls. Now that they can walk, Manuel goes off in one direction and—bam!—Rafaela takes off in the other. Man, I'm telling you, I may be too old to be the father of twins."

Reuben asked Luis to repeat what he had just said. "I can barely hear you. We've got a bad connection."

"Sorry, I'm on my cell. I just caught a case and am at the crime scene—over next to FDR Drive."

"I won't keep you then. I was just wondering if you and Francesca could have dinner with us—any night this week."

"That would be great, Reuben, but I have a hunch this job is going to be messy and take some time. Victim's a girl in her late twenties, maybe early thirties. Looks like she was strangled. Body discovered by an observant runner about two hours ago. Problem is her ID is obviously fake—the kind of bogus driver's license the kids get and use to go drinking. She's clearly old enough to drink, so the ID doesn't make any sense. Hallie Miller, the 'license' says."

"Does she have an address?" Reuben asked.

"Affirmative. It says 220 East 69th Street. I radioed it in and it's one of those new ugly apartment buildings off Lexington, right near you. Something called the Ladbroke."

"Oh God, you're absolutely right. I know it well and it's truly ugly. Repulsive. It's the nastiest place in the neighborhood. Makes me sick to my stomach every time I go by it. Built by that TV glamour boy."

"Yeah, right."

"Luis, I'm sorry you're not available. Will you call me when you get free? We want to see you—and the twins."

"You may regret that, amigo. But, yes, of course, I'll phone you."

"Much love to Francesca. And good luck with your case."

"Sure you don't want to get involved? For old times' sake?"

"No, sir. Not on your life! I'm out of the detective business."

Finished with his duties at the crime scene, Bautista removed his jacket in deference to the unseasonably warm late-April weather. He climbed back into his unmarked black car, stretched out his long legs, and started the engine. Returning to his headquarters on East Twenty-First Street, he thought about the unlikely but warm rapport that had developed between the Bautistas and the Frosts. The two couples were at ease socializing together, often going to the ballet, to which the Bautistas had become devoted, possibly even addicted. Both Luis and Francesca secretly hoped that Rafaela would follow Cynthia's path as a dancer—and for that matter, they wouldn't mind if Manuel did as well.

Reuben and Luis had a special relationship based on their joint sleuthing. Despite differences in age and culture—a young, tall, handsome Latino and an aging, slightly stooped WASP lawyer—they had more than once proved the axiom that two heads are better than one. Luis recalled, with not a little wonder, how their skills and perceptions had meshed so well in the past.

Too bad Reuben isn't on board for this new case, the detective thought. He guessed that the victim whose body he'd just seen had a sad, banal New York story, repeated far too many times: the bright career girl who arrives in the City and then falls into the killing hands of a predator, often a demented one. Not a likely case for Reuben. And, besides, his "Not on your life!" disclaimer had sounded pretty definite.

Two

DANIEL COURTLAND

Reuben had not made any progress in filling the blanks in his engagement book when Daniel Courtland, an old friend and client, called. After pleasantries, Courtland explained that he was at the Marine Air Terminal at LaGuardia, having just arrived in his private Grumman GIV from Indianapolis, and that it was "urgent" that he see Reuben.

"Can we have dinner?" he asked.

"That would be fine, Dan. I'm free."

"Good. It's really important. Six thirty at the Four Seasons." (Courtland always ate early—"on farmers' hours" as Cynthia had once put it—and, when in New York, always at the Four Seasons.)

"And could you bring Cynthia?" he added.

The request surprised Reuben. The visitor must have something to discuss other than a legal or business problem if Cynthia was to be included.

"I'll find out, but let's assume that she can," Reuben answered. He nonetheless warned Courtland of his wife's difficulties with arthritis, in case she did not feel up to going out.

"All right. I'll see you—let's hope both of you—at six thirty."

*   *   *

Courtland Diversified Foods had been one of Reuben's largest and most lucrative clients when he had been in active practice. A billionaire more than twice over, Courtland had spent a modest inheritance to purchase a chain of midwestern grocery stores in a bankruptcy sale back in 1970. The conglomerate empire that became Courtland Diversified Foods grew and grew after that, largely through shrewd acquisitions by its principal owner: a cannery, at least three enormous Western ranches, a cereal manufacturer, a frozen food maker—even a noodle factory in Brooklyn. At the current market, CDF shares were worth sixty dollars each and Daniel Courtland owned forty million of them, or thirty percent of the total outstanding.

Courtland considered himself the embodiment of the American dream—hard work leading to financial success and power. It had never occurred to him that he might not have made it if he had not received a million-dollar inheritance from his father. No, in his certain view, CDF had prospered through a combination of his own cleverness and the Free Enterprise System—with the capital letters he always seemed to emphasize when discussing it. By "Free Enterprise System" he of course meant a paradise with a minimum of union power, taxes, and government regulation.

Chase & Ward became CDF's lawyer at the time of the initial public offering of the company's stock. The corporation, while enormous, had been run largely out of Daniel's hat; the investment bankers bringing the enterprise to market wanted the business put in good order, and hoped that its owner could be instructed on the basics of good corporate governance. The lawyers at Chase & Ward were expert in such matters, and Reuben had been a Princeton classmate of the banker in charge of the deal, so the business came to him. (This was in the days when the old-boy network still flourished.)

Instructing Courtland in the ways of modern public companies was not easy. "Why can't I go after price cheaters?" He had protested, for example. (That is, why should the antitrust laws prevent him from fixing retail prices with his wholesalers and retailers?) Reuben had been patient with his pupil and believed, correctly as it turned out, that he would follow good corporate practices even if he was not convinced of their efficacy.

The offering was successful and Courtland retained Chase & Ward, and Reuben, as the lawyers for CDF on a regular basis. He also moved his personal business to the firm, becoming the largest client of Chase & Ward's principal trust and estates partner, Eskill Lander.

Courtland was some twenty years younger than Reuben, so there was a literal generational divide between them. There had never been a figurative one, however, as they seemed to complement each other nicely, though they were quite different: Reuben was calm, collected, and open; Courtland was instinctive, closed minded about many things, and short tempered. In fact, CDF's CEO was notorious for his short fuse. Reuben had observed it over the years as, for the most trivial reasons, the billionaire fired loyal subordinates, advertising consultants, and even the bankers that had originally steered him to Frost. He was also abrupt, if not downright rude, to secretaries and staff and, Reuben was forced to admit, his late wife, Gretchen.

Reuben always remained in his client's good graces, no matter how much he and Dan argued over an issue. Nonetheless, he warned his younger partner, Hank Kramer, when he took over the CDF account at the time of Reuben's retirement, and Eskill Lander, when he became the man's T & E lawyer, that their client needed to be handled carefully if they wanted to keep his business.

One reason the two men's relationship worked was because they scrupulously obeyed the old injunction to avoid discussions of politics or religion. Reuben, despite his eminence in a relatively conservative law firm, unashamedly called himself a liberal; Courtland was a thoroughgoing conservative. He was also a deeply committed fundamentalist whereas Reuben was an Episcopalian, his religion lightly worn.

But while he had certainly known of Courtland's right-wing bent, Reuben had only recently discovered—through a Google search—how different his own views were from those of his client.

Reuben had long been a Luddite as far as modern technical devices were concerned—still was, with regard to cell phones and BlackBerry smartphones, which he considered to be "enslaving"—but he had become a computer enthusiast once the young information technology specialist at Chase & Ward had taught him the basics.

"My God, it seems to me that a young lawyer could do everything—research, writing, communicating, et cetera—right from his desk without ever getting up," he had remarked at the time. "Not that that's necessarily a good thing—paunches and large rears are never attractive—but it certainly could be done."

Now his email correspondence was quite prodigious, his "address book" long; as an enthusiastic new convert, he had only contempt for his elderly contemporaries who refused to deal with the computer.

Reuben took a special delight in Googling; he found it much more entertaining—and more informative—than any gossip column, though he often shook his head in disbelief as he reminded himself that the verb, *to Google*, and the system itself, had not even existed a generation earlier.

On one of his idle days at the office he had Googled Daniel Courtland. He was shocked to learn the depth of his old friend's conservatism: a major supporter of the National Rifle Association and the American Enterprise Institute. Plus a very long list of conservative political candidates to whom he had made donations. And the Daniel S. Courtland Professorship of Ethics and Philosophy at Jerry Falwell's Liberty University, a benefaction he had never told Reuben about.

Frost was taken aback. However, he saw no reason to change his long-held view that Daniel Courtland, whatever the peculiarities of his personal views, was law-abiding and ran an honest company; there was no reason to dismiss him as a client. The Google search also showed the extent to which Courtland was involved in Indianapolis auto racing. He had mentioned his enthusiastic backing of a driver and supporting team in the Indianapolis 500 many times before, but Reuben, having zero interest in the subject, had not picked up on it. From the search entries, however, it was clear that his client was deeply caught up in the sport and was the sponsor of a major contender in the annual Memorial Day race.

"Doctors minister to patients who have venereal diseases all the time," Reuben had remarked, when he conveyed his findings to Cynthia. "So I don't see why I can't represent a corporation run by a mossback. And have an ecumenical association with a Red Stater."

After his Google discoveries, Reuben was even more careful to see that the Frost-Courtland mutual non-aggression pact remained in effect. That pact had enabled their friendship to persist even after Reuben ceased looking after CDF's affairs. If anything, it had deepened since the death of Courtland's wife two years earlier.

Cynthia genuinely liked Daniel Courtland, though she was frustrated by her husband's constraints on discussions of politics when they were together. She was sure the man needed educating and she would have been more than willing to undertake the task if she had she not been forbidden to do so. Nonetheless, she was pleased when Reuben called her to relay the invitation for the evening.

"The Four Seasons, I suppose?"

"Of course. It's the only restaurant in New York he knows."

"Well, at least we're getting out. As I said to you last night—"

"I know, I know. Before Dan called, I did, in fact, make an effort to improve our social life. I called Luis and invited him and Francesca to dinner."

"And?"

"He's tied up with a new case that he thinks will keep him out of circulation for a while. A body dumped over by the East River."

"Nobody we know, I trust." Cynthia wanted to make sure this was not another instance of Reuben stumbling into a murder investigation.

"No, a young girl named Millard or Miller or something like that. But she was practically a neighbor, living in that awful Ladbroke House on Sixty-Ninth Street."

"Oh Lord. I went by it just this afternoon and thought again of that stupid developer who called it the 'Ladbroke,' probably thinking it was a fancy British name when 'Ladbroke' is really the name of the biggest betting operation in England."

"Well, at least he didn't call it the Parker-Bowles."

They agreed to meet at the restaurant at six thirty.

"I hope I have the milking done by then," Cynthia said.

Three

THE FOUR SEASONS

Daniel Courtland was already at the Four Seasons when the Frosts arrived, seated in the Grill Room. The industrialist's devotion to the restaurant had always puzzled Reuben, for the simple reason that, when in CDF's executive suite in Indianapolis, Courtland always had the same lunch every day, and insisted that everyone eating with him have the same: a nasty combination of roast veal (always overcooked) and creamed spinach. Courtland insisted that it was the most wholesome meal possible and that varying one's daily lunch fare was unhealthy. It amused Reuben to think what would happen to Courtland Diversified Foods if the whole nation were to follow its CEO's eccentric example.

As for the Four Seasons, Reuben suspected that Daniel had read about it in *Holiday* or some other now-defunct 1980s publication. Granted it was still moderately fashionable in New York, but no one had bothered to tell him that the Grill Room was smart only at lunch and that one ate dinner in the so-called Pool Room. The Grill was usually not fully occupied at dinner, and certainly not at his six thirty dining hour. When Reuben and Cynthia arrived, he stood to greet his guests: a man of medium height, spartanly thin, in a shiny brown off-the-rack suit that almost matched his wispy brown hair.

"Why do these billionaires always look like they've bought their clothes from the Salvation Army?" Reuben had once asked Cynthia. "Are they just cheap, unwilling to buy expensive outfits, or do they think it somehow protects them if their wealth doesn't show?" Neither Frost had an answer. Reuben thought about the question again now. Courtland had arrived on his private jet and was about to dine in one of New York's most expensive restaurants. So why the bargain-basement clothes?

"Hello, Cynthia," Daniel said, offering his hand (no air-kissing for him). "And you, too, Reuben."

They sat down, Cynthia and Daniel on one side, Reuben across from them.

"To what do we owe the pleasure?" Reuben asked.

Daniel's face tightened. "Wait until we've ordered. I don't want to be interrupted." He waved a captain over. The man presented copies of the giant single-page menu to each.

"You know what I want," Daniel said.

"Yes, Mr. Courtland. The steak tartare."

"This is the only place in this whole country where you can get a decent steak tartare," Daniel grumped, with conviction. "What will you two have?"

Reuben, who in the past had often eaten at the Four Seasons, knew what he wanted, too—the Maryland crab cakes. Cynthia opted for a veal chop. And all three ordered oysters to start.

"What do you folks want to drink?" Daniel asked.

Frost knew that Daniel was a teetotaler, out of religious conviction and not as the result of a twelve-step conversion from alcohol abuse. But from past experience, he also knew that his host was tolerant of modest consumption by others, so Reuben ordered glasses of Côtes du Rhône for himself and Cynthia. Had he been dining only with her, he would have ordered a full bottle of something fancier, and preceded the meal with a martini. But discretion prevailed.

"Now to get down to it," Daniel said as the captain went away. "My daughter, Marina, is missing."

"How do you know that?" Reuben asked.

"I haven't had an email from her in five days, and she always sends me at least a couple every day. She hasn't been answering her home phone or her cell phone, either."

"What about work? Is she still at that publisher, Gramercy House?"

"Yes, and doing quite well. She's an editor now."

"Did you call them?"

"Yes. She hasn't been in since last Friday. And they have no idea where she might be."

"Maybe she's out working with an author," Cynthia suggested.

"I suppose that's possible, but it's very odd she hasn't been in touch with me."

"Have you called the police?"

"Not yet. I wanted to consult you first. You know how much I hate publicity. Doesn't do me or CDF any good, and those damned stories speculating about my wealth can only tempt conmen and kidnappers."

Courtland was perhaps referring to the latest ranking in *Forbes* of the world's billionaires, which put him 369th (at $2.5 billion) on the nine hundred–member list.

"Your left-wing papers here in New York would have a field day embarrassing me again, if they could," he went on. The

Frosts let the remark pass without comment, though both knew that Daniel was referring to the carnival in the tabloid press two years earlier when his wife, Gretchen, died under mysterious circumstances. Only the final report of the medical examiner in Indianapolis calling her death a suicide put an end to their speculation that there had been foul play.

A huge plate of oysters was presented, accompanied by the captain's loving description of the provenance of each variety.

"Seeing that edifice of seafood makes you understand why I prefer this place," Daniel said.

"You certainly are a walking advertisement for it," Reuben added. "You should get a ten-percent discount like the journalists who eat here. All those journeymen from the left-wing papers," he added, unable to resist the gibe.

Daniel scowled, then pressed Reuben on the question of a discount. "Reporters really get a break here?" he asked, surprised.

"That's what they tell me."

"I'll have to ask Julian about that," he said, referring to the owner-manager.

Amid wrestling with his oysters, Reuben asked if Marina had had any trouble at Gramercy House.

"I don't think recently. When she first went there, she worked for an editor named John Sommers, who apparently feels he has *droit du seigneur* with each new editorial assistant—female, that is. Marina put him off and felt she had thereby delayed her promotion to editor.

"But now she and Sommers seem to work together, principally on Gramercy's biggest moneymaking writer."

"Who is that?" Reuben asked.

"Woman named Darcy Watson."

"Oh my lord," Cynthia said. "I know her from the Cygnus Club. She must camp out there, I see her almost every time I visit. She—"

Cynthia stopped abruptly, instinct telling her not to launch into a largely critical description of Watson. Instead, she asked Daniel if he had met her.

"Yes, indeed. Marina introduced us a couple of months ago and I guess I have to admit I've been dating—can one still use that word?—her ever since. Her novels aren't exactly my cup of tea, but I find her a very interesting person."

"I'm embarrassed to say I've never heard of her," Reuben admitted.

"Oh, come on, dear. You see the bestseller list every Sunday. There's almost always a Watson novel on it. When one fades, another one comes along. She has a real following for her books, which are mostly about families and their struggles."

"Marina, even if she works with her, thinks she's a pretty mediocre writer. But I've told Marina it's not such a terrible thing to have your leading author one who isn't writing pornography or pseudo-pornography," Courtland said.

"Does Marina approve of your 'dating'?" Cynthia asked.

Courtland hesitated. "I'm not sure, Cynthia. But I hope she does."

"What about her own dating?" Cynthia asked. "Does she have boyfriends?"

"None at the moment, I think. Or at least none that I know about. There was a fellow she was serious about a couple of years ago, but she chucked him because he turned out to be a fraud. She had him out to Indianapolis—charming young man, witty and intelligent—but she discovered he was lying about almost everything in his background, from his original name and his education to his bank balance."

"Speaking of that, I gather from conversations with Eskill Lander from time to time that Marina has a large trust fund. Am I right about that?" Reuben asked.

Before Courtland could reply, two waiters and a captain wheeled up a cart and began a theatrical production of preparing the steak tartare—salt, mustard, grated garlic and onions, Worcestershire sauce, and finely ground, deep red raw beef. It was served with a flourish. Courtland continued after the interruption.

"Yes, indeed. I set her and her half-brother up with a substantial trust about seven years ago. Eskill told me it was a disaster tax-wise, but I wanted to do it just the same. And knowing how those idiots in Washington go about things, the gift tax might have become even worse if I had waited.

"So I set up a trust for Marina and her half-brother, Gino Facini—that's Gretchen's son by her first marriage. I paid a huge gift tax, but I wanted to get them established so they wouldn't be bothering me for money every minute of the day. I put in a total of thirty million dollars. They received three million dollars when they became twenty-one—two for Marina and one for Gino—another three million dollars when they became twenty-five, and then the balance, whatever it might be—and it will be considerable, thanks to some shrewd investments—when they're thirty. One-third to Gino, two-thirds to Marina."

"May I ask why the different amounts to the two of them?" Cynthia queried.

"That's easy. Marina is my daughter. My biological daughter. Gino was acquired. He was part of the deal that came with Gretchen. Not my biological son.

"I wanted them both to work, even though I made them independently wealthy. That's been okay as far as Marina's concerned, but unfortunately not with Gino."

"What's the problem?" Cynthia asked.

"He seems allergic to work. And once he got his installment at twenty-one, he stopped speaking to me. I haven't talked to him in years."

"Where is he?"

"I don't know, Reuben. He calls himself an actor, or at least he did. Last I heard, he was right here in New York."

"Why are you on the outs with him?"

"I'm really not sure. I'm afraid we were strangers to each other, and he apparently resented his mother's marrying me. Also, he showed no interest in coming into CDF, so I guess I showed little interest in him. In addition to everything else— and most outrageous of all—he blamed me for his mother's suicide. Most unfairly, given her mental condition. He also had a nasty cocaine habit, you know. Picked it up at his fraternity in college. I dreaded the thought that he'd put his share of the trust moneys right up his nose. But last I knew, he was clean after a stay at Hazelden."

"Have you ever thought of hiring a detective to find him?"

"No," Courtland said coldly, his look hardening. "I've done all I need to do for that boy. He's old history, as far as I'm concerned. A person I want nothing more to do with."

"But Marina continues to work, even though she's now rich?"

"Yes, thank goodness. And she's very wise about money. As far as I know, her only real expense has been purchasing her condominium, which she did when she became an editor. Pretty fancy place in one of those new buildings up your way. Something called the Ladbroke."

"The Ladbroke?" Cynthia asked. "Isn't that where—"

Reuben gave her a look and cut her off. "Yes, it's a block from where we live."

"You know, Dan, you're quite right about this place. As always, the crab cakes were excellent," Reuben said rather loudly, trying to divert attention from Cynthia's aborted question.

The trio decided to forgo both dessert and coffee.

"What do I do now, Reuben?" Courtland asked as he waited for the check.

"I think we should pay a visit to that new apartment. And, with your permission, I'll ask a police officer I know quite well to join us. It may be the smoothest way of getting the police involved, if it turns out that's what's called for. The apartment should give us some clue. Why don't we meet up at our place at ten o'clock tomorrow morning?" Reuben said.

"Fine. I'm at the St. Regis, as usual. That will be a good morning walk for me."

In the taxi on the way uptown, Reuben said he had not wanted to speculate, or to alarm Daniel Courtland prematurely, but he thought there was a good chance that Hallie Miller and Marina Courtland were one and the same person.

"Two girls murdered or missing at the same time from the same apartment building. Seems unlikely, unless we have a serial killer on our hands. I'll call Luis when we get home. I'm awfully afraid a homicide detective is what's in order."

"Oh my, Daniel will be devastated if you're right," Cynthia said. "In the circumstances, I'm glad I didn't run on about Darcy Watson, even though she's a menace around the Cygnus Club. Makes her presence known with her deep, husky voice, usually at full cry. Not that she needs to say anything—she's well over six feet. Not to mention the exotic Indian outfits she always seems to wear. I believe they're called *salwar kameezes*."

"Where the hell did you pick up that little bit of learning?" Reuben asked his wife.

"Let's just say I get around. For your edification, the *kameez* is a kind of shirt and the *salwar* a kind of loose pants."

"I'll be damned," Reuben said.

When Reuben reached Bautista at home, he asked the detective to join him the next morning. Luis protested that he was completely tied up with the Hallie Miller case.

"I may be dead wrong, but I think coming with me in the morning would be time well spent."

"I don't understand."

"Never mind. Just take it on faith, or at least my say-so. And bring along whatever information you have on Ms. Miller."

"I don't get any of this."

"I think you will."

Four

RECONNAISSANCE

Reuben wanted to explain his Hallie/Marina theory to Bautista before Courtland arrived, so he asked the detective to come to the Frosts' town house at nine thirty the next morning. Always prompt, his friend arrived precisely at the requested time.

"Maybe," Luis said, when the hypothesis had been laid out for him. "It's better than anything we've got so far. And we ought to be able to cinch it when your Mr. Courtland arrives."

"How so?"

Luis produced a photograph of a young woman, rather pretty even in a blurred, black-and-white mug shot. "This was printed off the fake driver's license Hallie Miller had on her. If it's really Miss Courtland, her father can certainly tell us that."

"Of course. But let me do some preliminaries when he gets here. He knows nothing of my theory. We should be gentle if the facts are as we—or at least I—think they are."

Courtland arrived, also as instructed, on the dot of ten o'clock. Reuben introduced him to Bautista and the three sat down in the living room. The host offered the other two coffee, but they declined.

"Dan, I think you should know that Officer Bautista, who is

an old friend of mine, is a homicide detective. He is currently working on the case of a young woman, whose name may or may not be Hallie Miller, found dead over near the East River. You think she died when, Luis?"

"The best estimate is some time last Friday evening."

"You look perplexed," Reuben went on, looking directly at Daniel. "I can understand that. But it's possible that there *may* be a connection between this dead woman and your daughter. You see, both Ms. Miller, if that is her name, and your Marina have the same address—Ladbroke House." Reuben nodded to Luis; it was his turn to continue the narrative.

"Mr. Courtland, I think we can clear this up very quickly. I have here a picture of the woman who was murdered—strangled—and left near the FDR Drive. May I show it to you?"

"Of course," Courtland said hoarsely.

"Take a look and tell us if this is your daughter."

Courtland glanced at the picture he had been handed, threw it down on the coffee table in front of him, and turned away, his mouth open wide and breathing deeply and quickly.

"Yes. That's her. No question about it. But why in the name of heaven was she murdered?" He spread his arms outward in a gesture of despair. "And why was she using an assumed name? And who, who . . . could have done such a thing?"

"That's what Detective Bautista and the police aim to find out. And Dan, my old friend, I'm very sorry at this turn of events."

"If you'll excuse me," Bautista said, "I'm going to call our forensic squad to meet us at your daughter's apartment. I don't know what we'll find there, but we want to preserve any clues that exist."

After Luis had left the room, Daniel burst into tears. "I can't believe this. My daughter was too smart to put herself in danger. Didn't that cop say she was strangled? What kind of fiend would do that?

"Reuben, I don't mean to sound sappy, but she was the love of my life—beautiful and smart and really caring about others. With Gretchen gone, and my stepson, Facini, a lost cause, she was all the family I had. It's not fair. Why is God punishing me this way?"

"I know it's unfair, Dan. But I can't answer your question about divine retribution. My only suggestion is that we, you and me, do everything we can to help Luis and his colleagues find the killer."

Bautista returned and explained that the forensics squad was already on the way to the Ladbroke. "Before we go, I'd like to get some basic information, if you don't mind, Mr. Courtland."

"No, go ahead. Ask whatever you want," Daniel said, slumping in his chair.

Luis, notebook in hand, drew out Marina's basic statistics from her grieving father, and where she had gone to school and where she worked. Daniel was less helpful in describing the details of her life in the City.

"As far as I know, she was moderately religious—or at least she was around me. And I don't believe she smoked or drank. At least she had the good grace never to do so in my presence. And unlike her half-brother, I'm sure she never used drugs."

Gino Facini's drug use led to a series of questions about him. Bautista wrote down, with a question mark, that he might be in New York.

"What about male friends?"

"As I was telling Reuben last night, she had a boyfriend a couple of years back but got rid of him."

"Why?"

"Because she found out he was a fraud."

A colloquy ensued about Marina's trust fund and financial independence. The one-third/two-thirds division between Marina and Gino was explained.

"In other words, there wasn't an even split between the two?" Bautista pressed.

"That's right."

"Interesting." The detective paused, tapping his pen on his notebook. "Getting back to the boyfriend, do you remember his name?" he continued.

"I believe it was Joshua Rice, though I only met him once. And I have no idea whether he's still here in Manhattan or what he does. As near as I could tell, he was unemployed when he was going with my daughter."

"Anything else occur to you that might be helpful?"

"Nothing that I can think of. Sorry."

Within the hour the three men had walked to the Ladbroke where three plainclothes officers, carrying a variety of forensic equipment, awaited them in the garish lobby. A nervous-looking building superintendent, Dristan Kovafu, was with them. (Kovafu was a full-fledged American citizen, but his youthful experience under the Hoxha dictatorship in Albania had made him instinctively nervous around policemen.)

The newcomers shook hands all around and mumbled greetings. Together, they took the elevator to the eighteenth floor and Marina Courtland's apartment, which the superintendent opened and then tried to leave. Luis stopped him and, after warning Reuben and Daniel not to touch anything, quizzed the super about any information he had about Marina and her habits and friends. His lack of knowledge turned out to be total.

The apartment was in pristine order—dishes done, clothes hung up, the two bathrooms clean. It could have been the digs of any moderately successful New York career woman, except, perhaps, for the signed prints on the wall—a Jasper Johns, a Howard Hodgkin, and a James Siena among them.

A silver tray of liquor bottles, in varying degrees of emptiness, was on a breakfront in the dining room. So was the only unclean object visible—an ashtray with three cigarette butts, each with a lipstick smudge on the filter tip. Reuben noticed it and reached the easy conclusion that Marina was not averse to either drink or tobacco.

Daniel noticed the bottles and ashtray, too, and looked surprised. "Never saw them here before."

Reuben stayed quiet, guessing that Marina had hidden any offending bottles and any evidence of smoking when her father had come to visit.

"Marina was always the neat one in the family," Daniel mumbled to Reuben as they wandered around, trying to keep out of the policemen's way.

In what Daniel called the library, they spotted a laptop up and running on a table next to a desk. Daniel leaned over and was about to use it when Reuben restrained him. "No touching, remember."

A detective came in at that point, surveyed the computer, turned it off, unplugged the DSL connection, and prepared to remove the machine. They watched as he opened the adjoining desk and tagged and bagged an address book and an engagement calendar. They also saw him pick up—wearing rubber gloves—a paperbound volume marked UNCORRECTED GALLEYS. They could see the title, *Carry Me Back*, and the name of the author, Michael Oakley. As the officer flipped through the pages, they also caught sight of several pages underlined with a bright yellow marker.

"You've been here many times?" Luis asked Daniel as they met in the living room.

"Not many. Half a dozen, maybe."

"Do you see anything different, strange, or out of order?"

"No. But I can't say I'm thinking very clearly just at the moment." He did not mention the liquor bottles or the ashtray.

"I understand. Maybe you should leave. We've got some more routine stuff to do, like dusting for fingerprints, but there's no reason for you to stay around for that."

"I think I'll follow your advice."

"I also want to talk to the doormen, both day and night, to see what they have to say," Luis added.

Reuben and Daniel left.

"I'm going back to the hotel," Daniel said as they went down in the elevator.

"Do you want some company, Dan?"

"No. I'll be all right. I'm going to stay here until Marina's killer is found."

"That may not be today or tomorrow."

"I don't care. I can afford the hotel bill. I'll call you when I've absorbed today's news a little better. Just one question before I go: I know you have no idea who murdered my daughter, but why on earth was she using an assumed name?"

"If I knew the answer to that, I might know who killed her."

Five

ESKILL LANDER

Frost headed directly to his office after leaving the Ladbroke. Given the connection to the wealthy and controversial Dan Courtland, he was sure word of Marina's murder would be spread on the Internet and splashed across the remaining local newspapers; he must warn Eskill Lander, Courtland's personal attorney, of the threatening storm.

Lander, head of the Chase & Ward trust and estates department, tall and straight-backed, looked as if he had rowed with the Yale crew perhaps five years ago rather than the twenty-five it had actually been. He simply did not appear to be forty-seven with his angelic Nordic, not-quite-handsome face.

Reuben had interviewed Lander as a second-year Columbia Law School student when he came to Chase & Ward seeking a job. His record was impeccable—at the top of his class and an editor of the *Law Review*. Before that he had been an honor student at Yale, having gone there on scholarship after leaving a small town in South Dakota.

The one reservation Reuben had at the time was that Eskill was not a very broad-gauged person, despite his excellent education. He seemed totally absorbed in the law, without any evident outside interests. Reuben had been sure that would change once he had left school and began earning a salary that enabled him to explore and enjoy the good life in New York City.

He was wrong. Lander certainly paid attention to his career, becoming a partner in a record six years, but Reuben, who saw him frequently at the partners' common lunch table at the Hexagon Club, had never heard him discuss or even mention a book he'd read, a play he'd seen, or a concert he'd attended. The man was totally preoccupied with his legal practice and his status as a much-admired expert on trust and estate matters.

Lander had a quietly assured manner with clients, but Reuben had always wondered if perhaps his partner was inwardly less self-confident and certain of himself than might appear. Unlike his colleagues, in his office Lander displayed framed diplomas from Yale and Columbia and certificates attesting to his admission to the New York and Federal bars. Plus—and Reuben found this truly odd—another one stating that Lander's biography was included in *Who's Who in America*. Didn't these wall hangings evidence insecurity? A need for tangible confirmation of his status as an important partner of an important law firm?

The widows adored Eskill Lander, and he was also a hit with the old men who often, in an impotent, homoerotic—if completely unacknowledged—way felt attracted to youthful-looking and athletic types like Eskill. To those who knew him less well than Reuben, he projected strength and solidity—and wasn't that what the oldsters wanted in their attorney? In addition to brains, of course, which Lander had in abundance.

Reuben knew also that his partner was somewhat a victim of his own success. By tradition, Chase & Ward only made nominal charges for writing wills and giving advice while a personal client was alive. But after the client's death, the firm received substantial fees for winding up the estate. The only problem with this arrangement was the ever-lengthening life-span of the firm's affluent, well-cared-for T & E clients, the trend helped along by the wonders of modern medicine. The lucrative posthumous fees seemed to be delayed longer and longer. Several times, the partners had debated going to a pay-as-you-go basis for trust and estates work, but each time they had decided to stick with the traditional method of charging.

Reuben was well aware that Daniel Courtland's estate was the largest one under Eskill's care—with the highest expectancy for the firm when he died. After Daniel had decided to bring his personal business to Chase & Ward, he, the billionaire from Indiana, and the bright young lawyer from South Dakota had hit it off instantly, and Courtland's loyalty had never wavered.

While he was discreet about discussing it, Reuben had developed a modest dislike for Eskill's wife, Irene. She had a career as a highly successful investment adviser at the bicoastal firm of Upshaw & Company. Customers were attracted to her—not for her looks but for her tough and wise advice. Making a terrible pun, Reuben had once told Cynthia that the woman gave "shrew investment advice." She had also helped many charities grow modest funds into substantial endowments, and for this she was referred to in some circles as the "Queen of the 501(c)(3)'s," the reference being to the Internal Revenue Code section dealing with not-for-profit organizations.

Irene Lander did not suffer fools gladly in the investment world, nor in her social dealings. Reuben found her cold and humorless; there was also, he was sure, an angry resentment just below the surface over the extent to which men dominated the business environment in which she operated.

It was known that Irene was older than her husband, though the other wives at Chase & Ward who cared about such things could not gauge exactly how much older. Never a beauty, her sharp features were nonetheless interesting, at least until a disastrous facelift several months earlier, which it was speculated had been undertaken so that the contrast between her aging looks and the youthful appearance of her husband would be less apparent. Reuben had not seen the result, but his sources told him that her face now lacked any character or distinctiveness and was a bland expanse of tightened, wrinkleless skin.

"Her skin is so tight I don't understand why she doesn't squeak," Cynthia, who usually refrained from such catty remarks, had said to him after a charity lunch where she had encountered Irene. "She should have had her work done in Brazil."

Reuben went to Eskill's office rather than inviting the young lawyer to his own spare quarters. He seated himself in a chair under the *Who's Who* certificate, facing Eskill, who was sitting at his desk in shirtsleeves. Frost got down to business immediately.

"Eskill, I have some terrible news to report. News you need to be aware of. Dan Courtland's daughter, Marina, has been murdered."

"Jesus, Reuben! When and where?"

"I'm not certain about the where—she was found over by the East River but could have been killed any place. When? The police think last Friday."

Frost went over the details and then asked Lander if he could offer any explanation for the Hallie/Marina confusion.

"Absolutely none, Reuben. You know, I've never met her, though I did meet her half-brother once. What's his name? Facini."

"Gino Facini, I believe," Reuben said.

"That's it. Anyway, as I've told you before, Dan insisted on setting up a substantial trust for Marina and this Facini. Both of them are now over twenty-five, so they've received what were the first two installments. The only things left are the residual payments—big ones—after they both reach thirty."

"And there's a two-thirds/one-third split between them, correct?"

"Yes.... And that's what brought about my only contact with Facini. He came to see me a year or so ago and said he thought that the two-thirds/one-third split was unfair and asked if there was anything that could legally be done about it. The answer, of course, was no. I also told him that he was lucky to be cut in for a third, since many stepparents make no provision at all for their stepchildren. He was furious at me and went away angry.

"As for Marina, as I say, I've never met her. Corresponded with her—we've even been on a 'Dear Eskill/Dear Marina' basis—but that's the extent of it. No personal contact. Just family business."

"Dan got along with her, didn't he?"

"I've never heard anything to make me think otherwise. Do you know something I don't?"

"No, no, I was just asking out of curiosity."

"What can I do?" Lander asked.

"Well, Dan is at the St. Regis, and I'm sure would welcome a call, or a visit. Or maybe you could bring him some veal and spinach."

"Oh no, Reuben, please."

Frost had one more question. "Any theories as to who might have done this?"

Lander replied that he did not. Then after hesitating, he added: "I do have one thought. I don't want to implicate anybody, but it could have been her half-brother. I'd always understood from Dan that he had a rather chancy record—dope—and he seemed a bit menacing, shall we say, when he came that time to see me. That property split certainly rankled. In addition, you know that he will get the whole corpus of the trust now that Marina's dead. Unless, of course, he's the murderer, in which case he'd be barred from taking her share."

"I don't want to think about that. But I'm not going to forget it, either." Reuben also made a mental note to convey the substance of his conversation with Lander to Bautista.

Six

THE DUTCH

In accordance with their let's-get-out-more program, Reuben and Cynthia had dinner that evening at a brand-new downtown restaurant called The Dutch. It was like old-home week for them as the chef, Andrew Carmellini, was a defector—after a couple of detours—from another favorite of theirs, Café Boulud, farther uptown.

The new restaurant catered to a younger crowd though, as Reuben pointed out to his wife, "At our age, my dear, almost any restaurant we go to will be catering to a younger crowd." Nonetheless, they were greeted warmly and seated at a table in the backroom, which was more intimate and less noisy than the busy area up front.

The place was crowded, the eaters plunging enthusiastically into Carmellini's offerings, both traditional and not so traditional. After inquiring from the waiter what *hiramasa* was and finding out that it was yellowtail, Reuben ordered it, while Cynthia settled for *barrio* tripe, made with beer and avocado.

When it arrived, the tripe was attractive, but not to Reuben. "You hate this stuff, don't you?" she asked.

"I don't know. I've never had tripe in my life and never want to."

"Open-minded as usual. Don't they serve tripe at that club of yours?"

"Yes, they do, but not of the sort you are talking about—or eating. Tripe used to pretty much describe the Gotham's food, but it's gotten better lately."

When Carmellini came by, they warmly congratulated him and praised the appetizers they were eating. On his recommendation, Cynthia ordered the rabbit pot pie.

"I've never heard of such a ridiculous dish," she told him, but nonetheless took his advice.

Reuben hesitated but finally asked for lamb-neck *mole*, convinced by the chef's enthusiasm for the dish.

"Lamb with chocolate sauce will certainly be a new one for me," he declared. He then toasted the good health of both his wife and Carmellini, raising the glass that sommelier Josh Picard had poured from the bottle of Saint-Estèphe he had recommended, Château Le Peyre 2005.

After Carmellini had moved on to another table, Reuben proposed a second toast. "Wish me and Luis Bautista luck. We'll need it if we're ever going to find Marina Courtland's murderer."

"Short of suspects?" Cynthia asked.

"Not completely. You heard Dan Courtland talk about John Sommers, Marina's boss at Gramercy House. He's a possibility. Then there's her half-brother, Gino."

"From what his stepfather said, he sounds like a bad apple."

"Eskill Lander seems to feel that way, too."

"Can you locate him?"

"We'll have to see. I think Eskill only has a bank account address."

"Didn't Daniel say he was a would-be actor, supposedly here in New York? Probably working way, way off Broadway."

"That's really supposition. Nobody knows."

"You know, Reuben, my young colleagues at the Foundation are unbelievable networkers. And most of them live downtown. If you get any kind of lead on Facini, I might be able to pursue it with them."

"Okay, I'll keep that in mind." Reuben was silent for a few moments and then resumed the conversation. "There's one other thing that I would never tell anyone else."

"I'm listening."

"Isn't it just possible that Dan Courtland was the murderer?"

"Darling, that's ridiculous. He's been your friend for years. How can you say such a thing?"

"I know, I know," Reuben answered defensively. "But I keep recalling the shadow that fell over him when his wife died. I know he was finally cleared, but there were still doubts, as you must remember."

"Yes, of course I remember. But what on earth would his motive have been?"

"Marina may have been jealous of his new tie-up with Darcy Watson. He hinted as much when we had dinner."

"I think that's pretty far out."

"Probably. But she may not have liked the idea of her father getting involved with a mediocre novelist. One must have standards, Cynthia. She also may have been worried that Dan would go gaga and leave the rest of his fortune to Watson."

"So when Marina objects, her father kills her?"

"Not very likely, I admit, but we have to consider all the possibilities."

"All right, if you want crazy possibilities, Darcy Watson may have been the murderer. Heaven knows that giantess could have overpowered and strangled Marina."

"Enough thumb-sucking," Reuben said. "But here's another question for you: What do you make of the change-of-name business? You really think Marina was concerned that young men would be after her for her money? And go to the length of using an assumed name?"

"I can believe it. People have ways of concealing things, particularly in a courtship merry-go-round. For example, if you were an accountant picking up a girl you wouldn't say 'I'm an accountant,' you'd say 'I'm in finance.' Similarly, I know that girls often call themselves 'actresses,' even though their day job has been waitress for a long time and they've never been onstage. One hundred percent honesty is not necessarily a feature of the mating game.

"And, Reuben, don't forget that your dear friend Daniel Courtland is pretty tight-fisted with money. Yes, he eats at the Four Seasons, but you've always told me he's close with a penny, at least in his business."

"Or when paying his legal fees."

"So his daughter came by her suspicions naturally. And she apparently had a bad experience with a gold digger. Gold digger—is that what they call the male variety of the species?"

"'Adventurer' is the male word, I think."

The two made their way through the meal and their bottle of wine but, as exemplary citizens, passed up having dessert and coffee.

"Cynthia, it's still one of the regrets of my life that at the age of seventy-eight I've had to give up coffee at night. I just can't sleep if I have an espresso after dinner."

"Lots of people drink decaf my dear."

"Lots of people are idiots. I only drink grown-up coffee."

"Well, at least you haven't given up gumshoeing."

"I like your choice of words. What I have done, and still do, is assist the police when I can, in those serendipitous circumstances that seem to keep arising. But on this one, I'm not sure I can help. Unlike General Westmoreland—remember him, from a war or two back?—I just can't see light at the end of the tunnel."

"Neither can I, but it's none of my business."

They restated their congratulations to Chef Carmellini, both noting that any doubts they had harbored about their unusual entrées had been pleasantly resolved, and left.

Seven

NEWS

Reuben was right about the storm that broke in the city's newspapers Friday morning. HEIRESS STRANGLED the front-page headline in the *Post* screamed. RICH GIRL'S VIOLENT END was the *News's* take. COURTLAND DAUGHTER FOUND SLAIN was the *Times's* more sedate reaction. None of the coverage contained any speculation about the probable killer or a motive.

All three publications pointed out that the body had been in its resting place for several days and that the dead woman was the daughter of Daniel Courtland, "the reclusive Midwestern billionaire" and "well-known conservative" (the *Post*) and "right-wing biggie" (the *News*). The *News* also mentioned the earlier suicide of Daniel's wife, noting that "this is the second time the tragedy of violent death has come to the billionaire's doorstep."

The *Times* focused on the victim herself, quoting John Sommers of Gramercy House to the effect that she had been a "brilliant young editor who would be much missed by the publishing house" and whose death came "as a total shock."

No account mentioned the initial Hallie Miller puzzle that

Daniel Courtland's identification had solved; the police had withheld that information.

"Dan's going to be fit to be tied," Cynthia Frost told her husband as they ate breakfast and read the news accounts.

"It could be worse," Reuben observed. "If the papers hadn't been so preoccupied with Dan, there could have been tiresome discussions about rape, the inherent unhappiness of the rich, and God knows what other nonsense."

Daniel himself called before they had finished eating.

"I've checked with that Bautista fellow and they are through with me," he explained to Reuben. "I'm going back to Indianapolis. Somehow the press jackals have found I'm at the St. Regis and have been hounding me. I've had the operator cut off their calls to my suite, but now there's a TV crew downstairs. Fortunately, they didn't recognize me when I went out for breakfast or when I came back. This is no place for a sane person."

"I can't say I blame you," Reuben replied.

"It's worse than the feeding frenzy back in Indiana when Gretchen killed herself."

Courtland asked for Reuben's cell phone number so he could keep in closest touch.

"Can't help you," Reuben grumbled. "I refuse to have one of those things." He was going to call cell phones "the work of the devil," but then checked himself because he might offend his straitlaced religious friend.

"Good for you. I only use mine in emergencies."

Reuben sighed to himself. How many cell users excused themselves by saying they used them "only in emergencies"? Walking down any New York street seemed to indicate the existence of many, too many, "emergencies."

"Do you think I can ask Eskill Lander to supervise getting

Marina's body back to Indianapolis? I understand it may be a couple of days before the medical examiner's office releases it."

"Of course. You want to call him or should I?"

"I'll do it. My daughter, after all."

Daniel added a final admonition to be notified "immediately" if Reuben heard anything new. "I'll be running around a lot the next few days—getting ready for the 500—but you can always reach me on my cell. And for heaven's sake, Reuben, don't give out my number to any of those press people."

That afternoon, Luis Bautista called.

"The computer guru here has been playing with Marina Courtland's laptop. He's found some pretty interesting emails. Can I come over?"

"Of course."

The two men sat down in the Frost living room an hour later.

"Our guy's still working on her machine, but what do you think of this?" He produced several sheets of printed-out material and handed them to Reuben. The first was an email from Marina to John Sommer.

"He was her boss, I believe," Reuben observed. "Or at least a colleague." The message, dated ten days earlier, read:

John:

I'm sorry to have to resort to email to call your attention to the Darcy Watson plagiarism problem. But since you refuse to discuss the matter in person, I have no choice but to put my position in writing. As I have now told you three times, Darcy Watson is a plagiarist. I know she is the house's leading author (and moneymaker)—and the biggest diamond in your crown—but Gramercy simply cannot publish a work that contains lifted material. (I have no idea about plagiarism in Watson's earlier bestsellers, so I'm only speaking about the new novel, *Carry Me Back*, where I, frankly, have caught her dead to rights.)

As you know, since you hired me, though you may not remember it, I wrote a senior paper at Brown on the 1930s magazine fiction of some of our more famous writers, including Faulkner, Hemingway, and Fitzgerald. In my research, I went through dozens of back issues of *The Saturday Evening Post* and *Collier's*. When I read the proofs of Watson's new novel, something struck a bell in her homey chapter on a country Christmas during a blizzard. I went back and found a story by one Gere Dexter in a 1938 issue of *Collier's*; it's almost word for word the same as the episode in Watson's book. I've sent you a Xerox, but you seem to have ignored it.

I know you said the "coincidence" was a "detail" and one no one without my special knowledge was likely to pick up. But that's a dangerous game and, even though I'm a relative newcomer here, I can't let Gramercy's reputation be endangered in this way. You have to confront Watson. As I told you, there are other "folksy" chapters in the book that sound like 1930s magazine fiction but which I have not been able to trace. She may be the favorite novelist out there west of the Hudson, and the firm's biggest helping of bread and butter, but you can't let her get away with dishonesty.

Since you refuse to talk with me any further about this, let me (and I'm most unhappy to have to do this) give you an ultimatum: either confront, or at least agree to confront, Watson by the end of the day Friday or I will take this matter right to the top, to Ray Greene. Understood?

Marina

"Hmmm. Pretty damned interesting. Was there any reply?"

"No."

"Further messages from her?"

"Just one, dated Friday, just a week ago, that reminded Sommers he had until the end of the day to comply with her request."

"That's some timing. A message like that from Marina and hours later she's dead. What's the next move?"

"Looks like we need to have a talk with Mr. Sommers. You want to come along?"

"I don't see how I appropriately can."

"We'll just say you're the late woman's lawyer."

"Stretching things a bit, but all right. I certainly want to."

"Let's end Mr. Sommers's week with a bang. I'll try to set it up for first thing tomorrow morning."

"Should be interesting."

"Interesting and maybe dispositive," Luis replied.

Eight

JOHN SOMMERS

Before meeting Luis on Friday, Reuben Googled John Sommers, marveling once again, as he did each time he connected to the search engine, how extraordinary it was to have all that information at his fingertips.

The entries for "John Sommers" were numerous. Reuben learned that he had been the subject of a recent *Publishers Weekly* profile of the "four hottest editors in American publishing." The article linked him to another concerning the bestselling Darcy Watson, incredibly described in *PW* as the "post-modern Booth Tarkington," whatever that meant. It also listed Sommers's comfortable stable of other authors, novelists, and a poet or two, several of them well known.

Google also served up a biographical entry that told Reuben that Sommers was forty-two; born in Harrisburg, Pennsylvania; educated at Johns Hopkins and Dartmouth (PhD in literature); and married and divorced before he was thirty.

A couple of calls to friends in publishing informed him that Sommers was well known in book circles as an energetic ladies' man and seducer. He was rumored to have been spared harassment lawsuits at Gramercy House in at least two instances only by making cash payments. And close involvement with Darcy

Watson, although she was at least ten years his senior, was also a topic of gossip.

Reuben relayed his findings to Luis when they met at four o'clock outside the Gramercy House headquarters in the new but unsightly building in the reconstructed Times Square.

"Times Square used to be the home of obscenity in the form of pornography," Reuben observed as they entered the building. "Now it's obscenity in the form of new architecture."

The reception area of the publisher, which more resembled the interior of a trendy airport terminal than a corporate head-quarters, had a commanding eastward view of midtown. They were shown to Sommers's large corner office, where the view was even more spectacular, looking both east and south.

A police detail had already visited the offices that morning, but had not seen Sommers. The policemen's task had been to inspect the cubicle where Marina Courtland had worked. The police operatives had carried off the contents of her desk and her modest files, though they had not had time to examine what they had taken away.

"This is getting to be a popular stop for you fellows," Sommers said to Bautista. "I hope, by the way, I can get out of here in time to get the 7:11 train to the Hamptons. I was going to take the 3:58, but so be it." He was not happy. Then, focusing on Reuben for the first time, he glanced quizzically at him.

"This is Reuben Frost, a partner in the Chase & Ward law firm and an attorney for Miss Courtland's family."

Reuben did not elaborate on—or correct—the description.

"Pleased to meet you, Mr. Frost," Sommers said, without giving much evidence that he was indeed pleased.

"I'm a bystander. Just here to listen," Reuben said. Sommers did not look convinced.

"I can't tell you, Mr. Frost, how shocked and sorry we are about Marina. Everybody here adored her—kind, smart, funny. I'm still not able to believe that she was murdered. Horrible. Just horrible."

"She wasn't here on Monday," he added. "We didn't think anything of that, since she often worked at home. We did begin to worry on Tuesday when she didn't show up or answer her phone."

"You didn't call the police?" Bautista asked.

"No, no. We didn't have any reason to suspect trouble."

"Except that she'd been missing for at least two days?"

"She was a grown woman, Detective Bautista," Sommers said testily.

"Let me ask a few more questions if you don't mind," Bautista continued, pulling out his notebook for the first time. "Anything else you can tell us about her?"

Sommers heaped even more praise on the dead woman. In addition to the many virtues recited, she apparently had real promise as an editor.

"Let me give you one anecdote. New assistants here are always stuck with the slush pile. You know what I mean by the slush pile?"

Reuben nodded affirmatively. Luis did not, so Sommers turned to him and explained that the slush pile consisted of manuscripts sent unsolicited through the mail or arriving "over the transom, so to speak."

"Marina found this wonderful manuscript in the slush pile—by a new novelist, Genny Josephs, called *Weatherman*, about the troubles of 1968."

"I've heard of it," Reuben said. "But haven't read it." He didn't add that it was hardly the type of fiction that might tempt him.

"Big success, as you may know, Mr. Frost. It made her reputation here. Going to be a movie, too."

"About Marina," Bautista interrupted. "You say everybody liked her. She didn't have any enemies here?'

"None that I know of. Certainly none that would be likely to kill her."

"How about male friends?

"I'm sure she had them. But I never met one. Our relationship was strictly professional."

"You never were involved with her socially?" Luis asked, armed with the insight Reuben had given him about the man's dalliances.

"No, nothing out of the ordinary."

Knowing that "ordinary" might have a special meaning for Sommers, Bautista asked specifically, but in a soft voice, if he had ever had any sexual involvement with Marina.

"That's a very personal question, Detective, and I rather resent it. But the answer is a very firm and definite no."

But not for want of trying? thought Luis, but discreetly refrained from saying so.

"How about disgruntled authors? Angry agents? Anything like that?" Reuben asked.

"Sounds like you know something about the publishing business, Mr. Frost. But the answer is no."

"Let me ask a question about you, Mr. Sommers," Bautista continued. "Where were you last Friday evening when Miss Courtland was murdered? April twenty-seventh? Exactly a week ago?"

Sommers once more looked nervous at the query, but again quickly recovered.

"As I nearly always do, I took the 3:58 train to Bridgehampton, where I have a little place, and stopped for an early dinner at

Almond, a local restaurant on the Montauk Highway, just after six o'clock. Then I went home, probably about eight or eight thirty and, being the workaholic I am, read a manuscript until bedtime."

"Did you eat alone?"

"Yes, as I often do on Friday evening. Just me and my martini."

"And then you went straight to your house afterward?"

"You mean, did I leave the restaurant, drive two hours to New York and murder Marina Courtland, take her body to the East River, and dump it before driving back to Bridgehampton and settling in for the night? Really, Detective, you're wasting my time."

"I'm sorry. But you were in Bridgehampton that whole evening?"

"Yes."

"Can anyone verify that?"

"Of course. Call Jacob Weiner at the restaurant. Or the taxi service that took me home after dinner."

After writing down the name and number of the taxi service, Luis thanked Sommers, closed his notebook, and made a motion as if to get up and leave. Then he produced a copy of the Courtland-Sommers email and said he had "just one more question."

"What can you tell us about this?" he asked, handing the copy to Sommers.

Sommers looked stunned.

"I'm sorry you found this. I guess there's no such thing as privacy these days."

Reuben and Luis waited while Sommers formulated a response, which he delivered in deliberate tones.

"I said I was sorry you found this, because it reflects badly on Miss Courtland. I tried to paint a positive picture of her for you and basically that portrait is a correct and accurate one. She did, however, have a stubborn streak. Often when she got an idea, she couldn't be persuaded to change it, no matter how convincing the arguments against it. Her charge of plagiarism against Darcy Watson was absolutely without merit. She's a totally honest woman I've known personally and professionally for many years. A completely upright lady, as you might guess from the type of books she writes.

"Marina took it into her head that Watson had lifted a chapter on Christmas in a rural snowstorm from some trivial magazine fiction written decades ago. Snow at Christmas, even heavy snow, is not exactly a copyrightable idea. But Marina got it into her head that Darcy was a plagiarist. And she was just plain wrong."

"Did you ever discuss this with Ms. Watson?" Reuben asked.

Sommers gave him a look as if to say he should leave questions to the police.

"In general terms, yes. I told her there had been a far-out accusation against her, but that she should not worry about it. I didn't mention Marina's name."

"Why not?" Bautista inquired.

"You may not know this, but Marina's father had taken up with Darcy Watson. I didn't want Darcy to think Marina was exacting some sort of revenge on her. I simply told her I would take care of the situation."

"Not by getting rid of Marina Courtland, I hope," Bautista said.

"Only in the sense that I was prepared to fire her. I trust, sir, when you said 'get rid of' you were not insinuating that I had anything to do with her murder?"

Bautista did not respond to Sommers's question. Instead, he

asked if there was an indication of how the girl felt about her father's new romance.

"It wasn't a subject she talked to me about. As far as I knew, she was approving, or at least not disapproving. Very possibly that changed when the plagiarism issue arose, but I really don't know."

"Do you have a copy of the *Collier's* story Miss Courtland referred to?" Reuben probed.

Sommers again shot him a mind-your-own-business look.

"She showed it to me, yes. But if I had it, I threw it away."

Bautista broke the tension by giving Sommers his card, with instructions to call him if any new thoughts about the murder occurred to him. Sommers was barely civil as they left his office.

"I think we caused some emotional distress in there," Luis said when they were back on the street. "And thanks for your help."

"I'm not sure Mr. Sommers would thank me. You think we'll see more of him?"

"Wouldn't surprise me," Luis said. "Meanwhile, I'll have the Bridgehampton types checked out. And also try to find Mr. Facini. Two leads are better than one, right, Reuben?"

"If you say so, Detective Bautista."

Back at the law firm, Reuben went to see Eskill Lander to recheck what information he had on Daniel Courtland's stepson.

"As I understand it, the only contact you've had with him was when he came to see you that time you told me about. When he wanted to crack the trust Dan Courtland had set up," Reuben said.

"That's right."

"And you have no address, no phone number, no way to locate him?"

"The best I can do is to find the address of the bank account where JPMorgan Chase wired his last payment."

"Where is the bank?"

"I'd have to look in the file. I assume this has something to do with his sister's murder."

"Yes," Reuben replied. "I'm afraid I've become a bit involved."

"Is that a good idea, Reuben?" Eskill asked, the tone of his voice indicating perhaps that he thought his colleague too old for meddling in such things.

"The homicide detective working on the case is a fellow I've known ever since Graham Donovan's murder here at the firm. And I really owe it to Dan to do what I can to help out."

"Have it your way," Eskill said, and then asked his secretary to bring in the Facini file.

"Here it is. The Bank of New York branch at Eighth Street and Second Avenue."

"And you're sure you have no other information, Eskill?"

"Wish I could help you, but no, that's it."

"Nothing about his so-called acting career?"

"Nothing, except his stepfather once said that's what he was supposed to be doing." Then he asked if Reuben really thought Gino had killed his half-sister.

"Who knows? But given his feelings toward her and the nice increase in his net worth that occurs if she's out of the way, he certainly can't be ruled out."

"Well, good luck. I guess we'd all be relieved if you and your detective friend can pin the crime on him. And I don't think Dan Courtland would be displeased, either."

Back at his own desk, Reuben checked the Manhattan telephone directory and information for a Facini listing. There was none. With his newly acquired computer skills, he also checked a website that searched out telephone numbers. Again, no success. And nothing on Google, either.

Then he called his wife to tell her that he had nothing to report except that Gino Facini had a bank account in a Lower East Side branch of the Bank of New York Mellon.

"I'm a jump ahead of you," Cynthia told him. She reported that both a boy and a girl in her office had a lead on Gino. If he had ever had success as an actor, neither they nor their friends had heard of it. But he seemed to be fairly well known as a performance artist with a pretty stable company called the Dockers, who appeared regularly in a loft on the West Side, overlooking the Hudson River. Further inquiry had determined that they were performing that very weekend, Friday, Saturday, and Sunday.

"You think we should go?" Cynthia asked.

Reuben groaned. "Well, we can't go tomorrow, with the damn firm dinner dance. But I suppose we could go Sunday. Not my idea of getting out more, but, yes, let's do it."

Nine

DINNER DANCE

The annual Chase & Ward spring dinner dance for the firm's partners was usually an event to be dreaded—it could be awfully boring—and yet Reuben now welcomed it as a possible diversion from the Courtland case.

At seven Saturday evening, the Frosts set forth for Cipriani 42nd Street, a catering hall that was formerly the headquarters of the Bowery Savings Bank. It represented the effort to import the Bellini (a drink of peach juice and Prosecco) and the unconscionably high prices of Harry's Bar in Venice to the Americas.

"If my late mother were still alive, and I told her I was going to a dinner dance in an old bank, she would have said I'd lost my mind," Cynthia said to her husband on the way.

"Especially if you told her they served drinks by the old teller windows and, I'll bet, use the vault as a wine cellar," Reuben added. "Or, more likely, to store the stacks of money the Ciprianis make in New York."

After arriving, Reuben and Cynthia moved toward the bar. The next forty-five minutes were spent greeting old acquaintances and meeting new ones. Reuben had been retired long enough that he was not familiar with many of the younger partners. Curious as always, he was glad to meet them and their significant others. He also noted that the firm had moved into the twenty-first century: There were three examples, two male and one female, of same-sex companions. Quite a change from the day when there were no women partners, let alone one with a female cohort. It quietly amused him to think of Judge Winkleman, a late federal judge and former partner, who looked down on Jews, Catholics, homosexuals, and immigrants and minorities of all colors and varieties, being asked to marry one of these couples.

Reuben, as a Venice devotee—if not exactly a fan of the Harry's Bar empire—liked Bellinis, even if they lacked the kick of his usual martini. So he downed perhaps more of them than he should have during the cocktail hour.

Needless to say, the crowd was abuzz with talk about Marina Courtland's murder. People assumed that Reuben, as the firm's sometime amateur detective, would be a source of information. He was quizzed repeatedly but managed to stonewall his questioners.

At the end of the pre-dinner socializing, Reuben and Cynthia found their table and discovered, to Reuben's dismay, that he would be sitting next to Irene Lander, Eskill's wife. (Years before, it had been decided that seating at the dance was too clannish and that the only way to mix people up was through assigned seating. Spouses, though at the same table, were not permitted to sit next to each other for the same reason. Reuben didn't know who did the seating arrangements, but once he had looked at the place card at the place adjoining his, he wished he could have had words with him or her.)

Mrs. Lander duly appeared, giving Reuben his first opportunity to view the facelift he had heard so much about. He almost didn't recognize her. The consequences were severe, tightening her face into an almost expressionless mass. Two other younger partners and their wives, the Wakemans and the Sterns, completed the table.

From past experience, Reuben knew that Irene Lander was obsessed with population control, contraception, and abortion, and that it was almost impossible to shift to other topics. She had even been known to discuss these matters with nonplussed young associates. Before he had eaten even two bites of his antipasto, Mrs. Lander began her spiel.

"Reuben, are you aware of what the FDA has ruled about the morning-after pill?"

"Irene, I can't say I am."

"It's disgraceful. The fundamentalists have taken over."

"I'm afraid Cynthia and I are beyond the age where below-the-belt issues are of much concern," Reuben said with a smile. "The only morning-after pill that interests us, or at least me, is an Alka-Seltzer tablet."

"That's ridiculous! *Everyone* must be concerned about these issues, about reproductive rights, about the population explosion around the world. If thinking people like you and Cynthia aren't involved, the right-wingers will take over. A disaster for women! A disaster for the world!"

As she went on, almost shouting over the very loud band, Reuben saw Cynthia wink at him from her place on the other side of the table. Glancing at Mrs. Lander, he uncharitably thought that she, with her newly tightened face, would probably not be able to wink at Eskill, sitting next to Cynthia.

Irene's apocalyptic preaching would have gone on over the veal scaloppini had Reuben not, as politeness demanded, turned to his other neighbor, the attractive young wife of Allen Stern, a young litigator that Reuben scarcely knew. They were able to discuss child-rearing, a subject of which the childless Reuben had no direct knowledge but did have a lifetime storehouse of remembered conversations. It was also a relief to discuss parent-hood rather than its prevention.

Then it was back to Mrs. Lander. In a preemptive strike, Reuben asked her about the state of the stock market and the view from her firm. She immediately launched into a lengthy explanation of her recent experience with derivatives, a subject Reuben barely understood.

Reuben wanted to get away. Perhaps he could excuse himself for a cigarette break, even though he did not smoke and guessed that Irene Lander may have known this. So he listened, or at least half-listened, to her demand to write the two New York senators about proposed legislative restrictions on Medicaid payments for abortions.

When Mrs. Stern returned, Reuben turned to her with relief and initiated a conversation about current movies. Then, as soon as dessert and coffee were finished, he said good-bye to Irene Lander and the other guests at the table. Just as he and Cynthia left, the band music changed from "old-fashioned" show tunes to a rock beat as unfamiliar to Reuben as the mazurka. (Cynthia could have handled it but, after all, she'd had a lifetime of dance experience.) The younger generation's notion of "music" now prevailed. Reuben was almost glad that Cynthia's ankle problem had kept them off the dance floor.

In the taxi on the way home, he began complaining about Irene Lander.

"I don't understand how Eskill puts up with her. She's a monster!" he told his wife. "She's like a broken record. All that Planned Parenthood stuff. Even if you're sympathetic, as I am, her harangue—which I've now heard at least half a dozen times—certainly puts you off. I tried to change the subject, but that got me into a worse trap."

"How?"

"I asked about her business and was treated to a lengthy discussion of her latest financial toy—called LEAPS."

"LEAPS?"

"Yes. Believe it stands for 'Long-Term Equity Anticipation Securities.' LEAPS."

"What do they do?"

"That woman talked so fast and with that band playing full blast, I'm not sure I can tell you exactly."

"Excuse me, did I hear you mention LEAPS?" their taxi driver asked from the front seat.

"Yes, I did," Reuben said.

"Greatest thing ever invented. Three-year options on stocks—puts or calls, you pick. Lets you get the upside from stocks without tying up all your money."

"There's your answer, Cynthia," Reuben said. "A better explanation than I could have given you."

"Yessir. I'm doing real well with my LEAPS on Merck and Walt Disney."

After looking at the driver's ID card in the window of the divider—for one Ahmed Jabbar—Reuben said, as he paid the fare, "Good for you, Mr. Jabbar. My congratulations."

"Best thing that's happened to me, sir. And thanks."

As he unlocked their front door, Reuben said, "That's the American way for you. Irene Lander and Ali Jabbar getting rich on LEAPS. What next?"

Ten

GINO FACINI

Cynthia, in her grant-making role at the Brigham Foundation, visited far-out performance venues searching for new talent. Reuben often accompanied her and patiently endured the privations involved. Invariably the works were performed in lofts up several flights of stairs. And these spaces always had the hardest wooden benches or chairs to be found anywhere. The pieces normally included angry rock or rap lyrics, performed at a volume rendering all but four-letter obscenities incomprehensible. There also always seemed to be the obligatory nude offering, with little lost ewes and lambs baring all to make a statement, though it was not always clear what the statement was.

Then there might be a genuinely funny skit, usually about a gender issue and frequently performed in drag.

"When it comes right down to it, I don't know why we're doing this," Reuben told his wife on their way to the Dockers' loft Sunday evening. He was having second thoughts about the wisdom of their venture. "It's not exactly as if I could go up to this fellow and say 'Aha! You murdered your sister!'"

"I don't think it does any harm to look over one more prospect—if you can call him that," Cynthia said.

The Dockers' loft was up only three flights, but that was enough to bother Cynthia. Once inside, on the predictably hard benches, Reuben was well aware that he and his wife were far and away the oldest members of the audience. Their presence was even more noticeable because the assembled crowd was small, not more than twenty people.

"I should have worn a backward baseball cap," Reuben whispered to his wife.

"And I suppose my midriff should be bare."

"A ring in your nose would have been better."

A girl led off the evening's program with a monologue about multiple orgasms, a heavenly state she declared she only occasionally achieved.

"I learn something new every day," Reuben exclaimed, again whispering.

"*Sssh*," came Cynthia's reply.

Then another girl, wearing a detachable pig's snout, a costume made of tinfoil, and illuminated fingernails that flashed on and off, sang an incomprehensible song that was either about animal rights or the joys of being a pig; perhaps both.

Eventually, without intermission, the finale, featuring Gino Facini, was reached. An emaciated young man draped in a bedsheet took the stage. He moved about very slowly, apparently in physical agony—and, judging by his expression, mental turmoil as well—as a recording of dissonant electronic music played in the background.

Reuben was sure he understood what was being presented to him: Facini's agonizing movements and the looks of pain and despair on his face were manifestly signs of grief, possibly for friends, perhaps a lover, who had died of AIDS. But Reuben was not as hip as he thought: The act turned out to end comically as the actor dropped his bedsheet, did a handstand, and revealed the true source of his distress—a fairly good-size carrot sticking out from his rear end. He pulled it loose to laughter and applause from the group around the Frosts.

"Pretty incredible," Reuben muttered.

"Agreed," Cynthia whispered back.

The Frosts went backstage with some trepidation, given Gino's reputation and what they had just seen of him—all of him—on the stage. But they felt that their scouting mission would not be complete without meeting the young man. They picked their way down the corridor that they thought led backstage and soon came to a ragtag room filled with discarded clothes, shoes, backpacks, stage lights, and a less than pristine bedsheet. Facini was in the middle of the mess, chewing out, in very angry terms, the fellow who had apparently been the lighting person for his act.

"Dammit, why did you sabotage me? The light at the end goes on my ass, not my face! Everybody's seen my suffering—now they must know *why*—the symbolic carrot—the Establishment, Jerry Falwell, Sarah Palin, Rush Limbaugh, all of them, giving it to me up the ass! How can I do the *symbolism* if you don't get the lights right?" He let loose with a stream of curse words that Reuben had not heard since his military days many years before. As for Cynthia, not at all unsophisticated herself, many of the epithets were novel.

"A new insight," Reuben muttered to Cynthia, as they overheard the outburst. "I thought it was all about AIDS, not right-wing politics."

"That's because you are sometimes behind the times, Reuben."

"Take a carrot and . . . No, no, that's too vulgar, forgive me." Reuben had almost gotten swept up in the volley of obscenities.

Facini interrupted his tirade to the hapless lighting person when he saw the Frosts. His look said, "Who the hell are you?" But his words did not. Being "ageist" would not have been correct behavior for a member of the Dockers—not that there was much occasion to be deferential to the elderly in their loft.

Reuben introduced himself and Cynthia. Facini understandably seemed puzzled. What were these ancients doing at his performance?

"I should explain that I'm a lawyer," Reuben said quickly. "My firm, and sometimes I, myself, represent your stepfather. And this is my wife, Cynthia."

"I see. Pleased to meet you." He smiled and held out his hand; the change in his demeanor was dramatic. "Thanks for coming," he added. "Hope you're not allergic to carrots."

The trio laughed, and then fell silent. Gino finally broke the silence by suggesting they go next door for a drink. The Frosts accepted and they were soon seated at an outdoor table at the Café Treviso. Gino had an iced latte and the two Frosts had glasses of Merlot, Reuben having discovered that the place had only a wine and beer license, which kept him from the stronger drink he really desired.

"I suppose you're here about my half sister," Gino said.

"That's a fair statement," Reuben replied.

"Well, I haven't a clue about what happened. All I know is what I read in the newspapers, as they say."

"I gather you weren't close to her."

"To put it mildly. Haven't seen her in, oh, at least five years. You probably know all this. After my mother died, I left Indianapolis for good, in part because I wanted to become an actor here, but also in part because my stepfather couldn't stand me. And I guess in part because I couldn't stand him.

"The final straw was when my mother killed herself. If that's what she did."

"Do you have any doubt about that? That it was suicide?"

"I prefer to think my stepfather killed her. Which he certainly did, indirectly if not directly. He was horrible to her."

Reuben was not entirely surprised to hear that Daniel had been less than an ideal husband. But he couldn't let the implication stand that the man had murdered his wife.

"You don't really think your stepfather killed your mother?" Reuben asked.

"No, I guess not. But I'm convinced he drove her to suicide. Which is just as bad. And which I absolutely do believe. He was always dissatisfied with her, critical of everything she did, the clothes she wore, the money she spent on the household. And he sure let her know it."

"I've always been told that Daniel Courtland never forgave you for not taking his name when you were adopted," Reuben said, shifting the subject to somewhat less contentious territory.

"That's right. My name's Facini, thank you. I was not about to change it, but my mother pressed him to adopt me anyway. He did—but you know about the financial settlement for Marina and me."

"I do. A trust fund: one third for you, two thirds for her."

"Correct. I can't complain. That trust money has kept me alive—more than alive, actually—while I'm trying to break into the theatre. But I can't forgive him for favoring Marina."

"You know, I talked to a guy at your firm about the legalities of what old Dan had done. He wasn't any help and I didn't find him very sympathetic."

"That was Eskill Lander, I believe."

"That's right. Who can forget a name like Eskill?"

"None of that matters now," Reuben pointed out. "The trust fund is entirely yours."

"Yeah, I suppose it is. Lucky me!"

Reuben ignored Gino's rather tasteless bravado. "Even if you weren't close, do you have any idea who might have killed your half sister?" he asked.

"None. As I say, I wasn't in touch with her."

"Does the name Hallie Miller mean anything to you?" Cynthia asked.

"Nope. Should it?"

"Your half sister used that name sometimes," Reuben explained.

"You're kidding. Why the hell did she do that?"

"Apparently, so people wouldn't know she was the Courtland heiress."

"I'll be damned."

"Maybe you'll start using the Miller name, now that you're the sole beneficiary of the Courtland trust."

Facini made clear that he did not think this was funny. Cynthia deftly changed the subject to gossip about the downtown theatre scene, but the coffee hour was soon at an end.

"Thank you for your time, Mr. Facini," Reuben said, after paying the check, thinking, with some amusement, that young Facini was now in a better position to pay it than he was. "And here is my card in case anything occurs to you that might help us find Marina's killer."

Reuben also took down Facini's cell phone number.

"Nice to meet you. *Ciao*," Facini said as they shook hands and parted. He crossed the street and, to the Frosts' surprise, unlocked a bright blue Jaguar and drove off.

"A struggling actor," Cynthia said to her husband.

"Yes. With a very comfortable trust fund," Reuben answered.

Reuben and Cynthia sat down over drinks once they reached home—a martini this time, not the Café Treviso's "so-called Merlot," as Reuben put it.

"Another interesting downtown evening," Reuben said. "But more important than the artistry, what did you think of Signor Facini?"

"He's a clever young man," she responded. "Not that it takes much inventiveness to wear a bedsheet and stick a carrot where it doesn't belong. But he's got the skills of an actor."

"How do you mean?"

"Let me get us something to eat and I'll tell you. Sandwiches all right?"

"Don't have much choice, I expect."

Then, over grilled cheese sandwiches and non-merlot, Cynthia explained herself.

"Start with the proposition that young Mr. Facini is supposed to be difficult, with a chip on his shoulder and a bad temper. At least that's the way both his stepfather and Eskill Lander describe him. And we saw evidence of that the way he was abusing his lighting man. He was prepared to treat us in the same rude way until he found out who you were. Then it was pretty much charm and sweetness."

"So? Where does that get us?"

"Probably nowhere, but he was eager to make a good impression."

"So we wouldn't think he'd murdered his half-sister in a jealous fit of rage? And driven her in that blue Jaguar out to the edge of the East River?"

"Maybe."

Eleven

A SURPRISE

Monday morning, the receptionist at Chase & Ward called to Reuben when he stepped off the elevator and told him that Russell Townley, the firm's new Executive Partner, wanted to see him "immediately."

"It's an awful shock, Mr. Frost," she said.

"What's a shock?"

"Young Mr. Joyner's death."

"Who?"

"You know, our associate, Mr. Joyner."

"I don't know anything about it."

"He was found dead in his apartment last night. At least that's the word going around."

"How terrible," Reuben told her as he went off to Townley's office as ordered, even before his morning coffee. A feeling of dread came over him as he walked down the corridor; if there had been foul play within the Chase & Ward family, the purpose of the Executive Partner's summons was surely to get him caught up in dealing with it.

He vaguely recalled Joyner—Edward Joyner he believed his name was—from one of the firm's annual outings for partners and associates. He guessed that he had met the fellow, but he had left no strong impression. If Reuben had the correct person, Joyner was a three- or four-year associate in the corporate department, too young to have been discussed for promotion at a partners' meeting.

Frost reached Townley's magnificent corner office—the traditional quarters for the firm's Executive Partner—and went in without knocking. He was amused, as he had been on previous visits, by the way the office had been redecorated to Townley's specifications—staid, proper, and uninteresting furniture and prints of Olde New York on the walls. Perhaps, Reuben thought impishly, to make clear to the world that Townley was of Olde New York stock. *Boring* was the word that came to Reuben's mind; the decor was totally unlike the sleek, Italian-modern furniture in his own office when he had been an active partner; the grandfather clock in the corner would never have been found in his quarters.

Townley, a rather small man in his late fifties, wearing a vest despite the balmy spring weather, jumped up from his desk to greet Frost.

"Thank God, you're here, Reuben," he said. Since assuming the post of Executive Partner from Charlie Parkes, the previous incumbent, three months earlier, Townley had seemed rather nervous and flighty. Those qualities were abundantly evident now.

"I have some terrible news—"

"I think I've already heard it," Reuben said. "The Chase & Ward jungle drums are already beating."

"Good grief, I only learned about this Joyner thing thirty minutes ago, when the police called."

"Russ, you know a secret can't be kept around here for more than a microsecond. Tell me what you know."

"A detective named Muldoon called me and said that our associate Joyner had been found stabbed in his apartment. That's it. No other details. However, he warned me that the police would probably be around to question people here. What do I do, Reuben? You've been through this before. Give me a clue."

"Yes, long ago and as recently as two weeks ago. You recall that Dan Courtland's daughter was murdered then."

"I suppose you're involved in that, you being Courtland's old buddy."

"I don't think 'buddy' is precisely the right word, but Courtland's certainly been a friend. And yes, I'm involved in the investigation of Marina's death. Peripherally, I hope."

"You're the firm's expert on murder. Vast homicide experience. We've got lawyers who know about tax shelters and suck-up mergers and document dumps and every other lawyer thing. But you're the homicide authority." He fluttered his hands as he spoke.

"I'd like to think, Russ, that my reputation at Chase & Ward has more to do with substantive matters other than random slaughtering."

"Of course, Reuben, of course," he replied, his hands still fluttering.

Reuben, given his long-retired status, had not had a voice in selecting Townley as the new Executive Partner. Partners over seventy-five did not have a vote, like cardinals over the age of eighty who did not have a vote in selecting the pope. He had, however, agreed with the choice, though the man's nervousness under stress was beginning to give him doubts. (His only other reservation had been Townley's lack of deference to Reuben and his other retired colleagues. It was paranoid to think so, but he had wondered whether Townley didn't perhaps wish that the oldsters would disappear—i.e., die—thus easing the burden of payments under the firm's generous retirement arrangements.)

"All right, all right, let's just say that your crime experience has been a *sideline*. What do we do? Help me out!"

Reuben tried to order his thoughts, as he always had over the years when confronted with any firm crisis.

"I take it we don't know any of the circumstances of this fellow's death. No idea who the perp—a word I've picked up in my 'vast homicide experience'—might be."

Townley gave a hollow laugh. "I know nothing other than what I've already told you."

"I assume there's no reason to think that anyone here at the firm had anything to do with this," Reuben asked.

"No, thank God. At least not anybody that I'm aware of."

"Did he leave a wife, a family, what?"

"I've got his personnel file here," Townley answered as he reached for the green manila folder on his desk and opened it.

"As near as I can tell, he has no relatives other than a father in Tucson. He did have a wife, but they had a very messy divorce two years ago. You know about that?"

"No."

"It was his personal fight, his personal business, but we had to get involved a little bit when the divorce mavens representing his wife tried to garnish his salary here. Eskill Lander—as you know, he's the closest thing we've got to a domestic affairs attorney—had to step in and fight them off."

Reuben was silently amused. Eskill, as the firm's preeminent trust and estates lawyer, had dealt with several prominent multimillion-dollar divorces, but always with immaculately clean hands, and never at the pedestrian level of garnisheeing a person's wages. It must have been quite a confrontation with the "divorce mavens."

"He'd married his wife before law school. Maybe you met her at one of our social events. Nice girl, as I recall. Foreigner of some sort."

"Not that I remember."

"Well, it seems like the classic case: Wife supports husband through law school, then gets dumped when hubby hits the big-time."

"What else does that file show?"

"Let's see. Young Joyner was born and grew up in Montgomery, Alabama. Public school there, then the University of Alabama and Tulane Law School. Did well there, which is why he ended up with us. Not exactly a law school on our A-list, but he came here four years ago when, you may recall, we had to reach out for new recruits. That goddamn article."

Townley was referring to an *American Lawyer* piece that named Chase & Ward as one of the nation's top three law office "sweatshops." It had put a temporary chill on the firm's recruiting efforts, but with the recent shrinking of legal openings, it was ignored—or never known—by the current crop of job prospects.

"He was assigned to the corporate department, and has not been a particularly distinguished citizen, I gather. I'm trying to get the scoop from Jerry Gilbert, for whom he most recently worked, but Jerry isn't here yet. One of our late-arrival gang."

"There is such a gang," Reuben agreed, having always been a member himself. The point was lost on the punctilious Townley.

"Where did he live? Where was the body found?"

"His address in the office directory is in Tribeca. Probably one of those lofts our overpaid associates can now afford. The file shows a change of address, which would indicate he moved there after his divorce. So much for the background. I go back to my original question: What do we do?"

"First thing, Russ, is get ready for the press. It's not every day that an associate of what they insist on calling a 'major white-shoe law firm' is murdered. Send out a memo that no one is to talk to the press except you."

"Why me?"

"Because, my friend, you are the Executive Partner."

"What do I say?

"Stick to the facts. When he was hired, what department he was in. Nothing about who he worked for. Nothing about the clients he did things for. And for God's sake, nothing about his ability or lack of it. He was an associate here, period. Not a good associate, a bad associate, a promising associate, just an associate. And a junior one at that."

"And can I count on you to do some sleuthing?" Townley asked.

"You'd better not. You forget how ancient I am, and I'm busy enough holding Dan Courtland's hand and assisting, as best I can, the police in the investigation of Marina's death."

Townley looked disappointed.

"Of course, just as a matter of my own curiosity, I may talk to Eskill Lander and maybe the partner Joyner worked for. Jerry Gilbert, was it?"

"Yes. I'll be grateful to learn anything you find out. And, Reuben, couldn't you be our liaison with the police? You know all the people down there."

"Again, no. I know one detective, who I doubt, from what you say, has anything to do with this case. I have no idea who this Muldoon fellow is. I simply can't devote time to this. But I assure you you'll be the first to know if I find out anything. And please feel free to call me at any point."

"Thank you—I guess."

"Just one other thing, Russ. I assume you can't see any connection between Marina Courtland's murder and this one?"

"Good Lord, no. What a strange idea!"

After a delayed cup of coffee, Reuben called Bautista to report on the encounter with Gino Facini the night before. The detective told him that there were not any new developments on his end, other than a nasty crack in a tabloid gossip column wondering why Marina's—the "moneyed Marina's"—killer had not been tracked down.

"I think we'd better have our own look at Mr. Facini," he told Reuben. "Where do we find him?"

Reuben gave him the address of the Dockers loft, along with a warning, which mystified Luis, to "watch out for carrots." Then he told the detective about Edward Joyner's murder.

"Homicide seems to be spreading over here like Asian flu," Reuben said. He told Luis that the case had apparently been assigned to a detective named Muldoon. Luis said he was actually in the next office; he'd talk to him and get back.

Within the hour, Bautista called. Joyner's body had been found in a pool of blood in the living space of his loft apartment, with multiple stab wounds to the chest. No sign of struggle, no sign of robbery or theft, no sign of breaking and entering. No obvious clues; the only theory was that the deed had been done by someone who knew the young lawyer.

"I'll keep in touch with Muldoon," Bautista promised.

*   *   *

Reuben paid a call on Eskill Lander once again, explaining that he wanted to inquire about Edward Joyner's divorce.

"You getting involved in this one, too?" asked Lander, in an exasperated tone that again implied that he thought that Reuben was a meddler. He complied, however, and got up and paced his office as he filled in the details.

"What a mess! Dealing with the divorce bar. Not a pretty bunch. Joyner had his own lawyer, but when his wife's attorneys wanted to garnish his wages and try to attach his assets under our firm's 401(k) plan, Charlie Parkes asked me to interfere. Digging into the facts, it seemed quite clear to me that Joyner was in the wrong."

"Russ Townley told me the wife helped him out through law school and then was dumped when they got to New York," Reuben interrupted. "An old story, that."

"Not quite the usual story in this case. She was the one who initiated the divorce when she found out he was carrying on with a young lady lawyer from the Lenox, Ashford firm. But she was not entirely blameless. She was a Brazilian—how he met her at the University of Alabama I don't know—and I suspect she married Joyner to get a green card. I also think they had grown tired of each other by the time of the divorce. But the adultery part infuriated the wife, and she was determined to make the whole thing as painful as possible for her philandering husband, financially and otherwise. And she did."

"Was it ultimately settled peaceably? Without litigation?" Reuben asked.

"Yes, after months of Mickey Mouse by her damnable lawyers. The striking thing to me was Joyner's attitude. He always acted like he was God's gift to mankind and had a self-righteous outlook on the whole proceeding. He never, never acknowledged his own misconduct. A real shit, in other words, dressed in rather flashy Paul Stuart tweeds. He also had a slight mid-Atlantic accent—rather strange for a white-trash boy from Alabama."

"What happened to the wife?"

"No idea. May have gone back to Brazil, for all I know."

"Well, *muito obrigado*, Eskill," Reuben said.

"Where the hell did you learn that?"

"Rio. Many years ago. It means 'many thanks' in Portuguese."

"*Mille grazie*, I never would have guessed it."

Twelve

A RESPITE AT THE CLUB

Reuben decided that, before questioning Jerry Gilbert, as he had told Russ Townley he might do, he needed a break at his favorite haunt, the Gotham Club—or, as his wife called it, his "tree house." He had come to use the Club at Fifty-Sixth Street and Fifth Avenue more and more in his retirement years. Despite his crack about the food there being "tripe," it had in fact improved considerably with the installation of a new chef. It was now much more appealing for lunch.

Bowing to civic pressure and the sentiment of most members—but by no means all—the Club had also begun admitting women, for the first time in its hundred-year-plus history. This had not troubled Reuben, who did not share the apocalyptic vision of some of his fustier club mates. Yet the new regime was a far cry from the day when the Club did not even have a ladies' room. "If we install a lavatory, they'll be here every chance they get," one old party had thundered when this radical proposal had first been made back in the 1970s. These days, any current member's retrograde views, assuming such still existed, were held in silence.

The decision to admit women did not really alter the customs of the club that mattered to its regular users, like the carefully prepared martinis of Renato, the bartender. Or the greetings of Jason Darmes, the doorman, who grew both more portly and more genial year by year.

"How are things, Mr. Frost?" he asked as Reuben entered, energized by a walk from his office in bright midday sunshine.

"Just fine, Jason," Reuben answered, knowing full well that the things that now concerned him most were far from being "fine."

Once at the tiny second-floor bar, Reuben ordered a martini.

"A Gotham?" Renato asked, meaning a martini with a "dividend" on the side, which made it two martinis by any rational reckoning.

"You keep tempting me, Renato. But my doctor says strictly normal size and only one."

"Coming up."

Reuben was pleased that there was one Gotham martini drinker at the bar, albeit a female foundation executive elected in the first wave of women members. By contrast, he saw that the three men present were sipping on white wine—a spritzer in one case, he noted with particular contempt. *O tempora! O mores!*

Drink in hand, Frost headed at once for the dining room, avoiding conversation with the other drinkers. He was not being antisocial but, given the imbroglios in which he was entangled, he was not eager to make small talk about what he was up to.

He sat down at the common table, reserved for those members lunching alone. Sitting there was often a perilous enterprise, since there were two or three extraordinary bores who appeared at the table with distressing regularity. He noticed one of them there today, with an empty chair beside him, so he quickly moved to the only other vacant place at the opposite end of the table.

But Reuben was wary when he took the vacant seat next to a woman he did not know. His apprehension proved to be unwarranted as his luncheon companion turned out to be Amanda Bretton, the dean of the faculty at a nearby suburban college. Conversation with her was easy, as it was with his other companion, Peter Day, a magazine editor he had known for years.

While the three were talking, Reuben heard Daniel Courtland's name mentioned by someone farther down the table.

"Awful thing about his daughter," Reuben heard.

Ms. Bretton caught the reference, too, and asked the speaker if he knew Courtland. The man said no.

"He's quite a case," Ms. Bretton said to the group. "When I was a dean at Indiana University, he revoked a pledge for five million dollars to our religion department because they wouldn't hire a professor he had handpicked. A very conservative and somewhat eccentric preacher with very little in the way of academic qualifications."

There were mild sounds of disapproval within the group and then the individual conversations resumed.

"I'm interested that you know Daniel Courtland," Reuben said to Ms. Bretton. "He was a client of mine for many years and is still a client of my old law firm."

"Should I say lucky you or poor you? I'm sure there's an immense amount of legal business. But our experience was not too pleasant."

"We have always had a tacit agreement—we never discuss politics or religion. I'm reasonably sure our views would be quite divergent."

"You've been wise. What about his daughter? Was she of the same persuasion as her father?"

"I'm not sure. But I should think not. The people at the publishing house where she worked seemed to think the world of her. I don't think that would have been true if she went around trumpeting her father's views."

"Well, anyway, it doesn't matter now, does it?"

"Sadly, no."

Reuben, having finished a quite decent club sandwich (he shuddered to think of the creamed chipped beef and other such fare that used to be available), excused himself and left the Club. The luncheon encounter had left him with two thoughts: Marina Courtland may have used her pseudonym not only to conceal her wealth, but also to prevent being identified with her father's opinions. And, while he knew that Dan Courtland was volatile, Ms. Bretton's evidence made it all the more necessary to handle him with care—or at least to handle the investigation of his daughter's death with care.

Then, as he reached One Metropolitan Plaza, he began thinking about his upcoming meeting with the Executioner.

Thirteen

THE EXECUTIONER

He may never have heard the epithet himself, but Jerry Gilbert was known among the Chase & Ward associates as "the Executioner." Legend had it that if a partner felt that an associate should be fired, but didn't have the courage to do the job himself, he would arrange to have the victim assigned to Gilbert.

This myth credited the partners with too much efficiency in handling their personnel matters. It did, however, reflect the basic truth that Gilbert was a stern and difficult taskmaster: laconic in explaining assignments, sarcastic when ripping apart written work submitted to him (nearly always returned bleeding with editorial corrections and queries), and stingy with compliments and words of encouragement.

Those who survived their assignment working for Gilbert felt like combat veterans. In the case of some, the experience developed them into tougher lawyers, but a few left as shell-shocked, nervous wrecks, including the ones "executed." At age fifty, Gilbert had a long career at the firm ahead of him; associates had hopes of avoiding his rough tutelage only through the luck of the draw, not because of the man's retire-ment or early demise.

Reuben knew of Gilbert's nickname, but had never been cer-tain how accurate the popular wisdom was. All he knew was that he did not especially like the man—nothing personal and he didn't deliberately try to avoid him—but Gilbert was pretty stony and humorless, and thus not to Frost's taste. A good law-yer? Absolutely. A lovable person? No way.

"How are you, Reuben? Haven't seen you upstairs at the Hexagon Club recently," Gilbert said once Frost was comfortably seated on the office's sofa. The Executioner took a seat in a chair opposite and put his feet up on the coffee table in front of him.

"I don't go up there as much as I used to. I feel a little bit in the way when I do. All the active partners discussing current business. The last thing they need is an ancient crock like me reminiscing about the good old days." *Or about the day Graham Donovan dropped dead at the firm's table at the Club*, Reuben thought.

"Nonsense. You're always welcome, you know that," Gil-bert said, giving Reuben a narrow, pinched smile—the closest he came to camaraderie. "To what do I owe the pleasure?" The pinched smile a second time.

"I understand Edward Joyner—the late Edward Joyner—worked for you. "

"Yes."

"I assume he was assigned to you to put him to a final test to make sure the firm was right to fire him."

"Not at all, Reuben. Joyner came to me with a decent repu-tation. He was a pretty good lawyer, just a little too much self-confidence. That was the verdict when he started with me."

"And?"

"And he was good—not outstanding, but good—until his divorce unstrung him. You know about that?"

"I think so."

"He started being consistently late for work, not that that's a capital offense . . ."

"Agreed. Only Russ Townley favors the death penalty for late starts in the morning, as I believe you, and surely I, know."

"Yes. But lateness was the least of it. His work became more and more careless, and he consistently missed deadlines. My discreet inquiries told me he was leading the club life. I don't mean the Gotham, Reuben, I mean those all-night coke joints downtown."

"I'm glad you don't think the Gotham is a drug den," Reuben said. He suddenly remembered with some embarrassment that Gilbert had been proposed for membership—and been black-balled.

"Quite the playboy, man-about-town, I understand. He had a messy little affair with a lawyer at . . ."

"I've heard about that."

"And, if the grapevine is right, at least an attempted fling with Arch Tanner's wife. I never delved too deeply into that."

"I've heard something about that, too," Reuben said. In fact, Cynthia, after a luncheon with several other Chase & Ward wives at their club—also not a drug den; a good Protestant, thriftily priced Muscadet being the strongest stimulant available there—had reported on a rumor that Isabel Tanner was seeing something of an unnamed associate at the firm. Reuben realized it did not have to be Joyner; there had been other social occasions during which Isabel's feminine hand had been a bit too careless up against an associate's brow or cheek—or even thigh.

In the name of discretion, Reuben did not make any comment about Mrs. Tanner's propensities; he was sure Gilbert, like everyone else (except, presumably, Arch Tanner) knew about them.

"So, Jerry, Mr. Joyner fell apart on you."

"Yes. He became completely useless. Though the extraordinary thing, Reuben, is that it did me absolutely no good to tell him so. I told him as directly as I knew how that he had no future here. He simply refused to take this in. Said he'd been through a bad patch and all would be well in the future. I told him point-blank that it was too late—too many marks against, but without mentioning specifically the hanky-panky stuff—and that he should be looking for 'other opportunities elsewhere,' as the saying goes."

"You really gave him an ultimatum?"

"Yes. Only about three weeks ago. I told him he had three months to find another job, then he was out."

"How did he react?"

"With the greatest self-confidence, he said that he would prove himself in those three months. He knew he was partnership material, he insisted, adding that he was sorry about recent difficulties. He would not only be a partner but one who would make us all proud."

"Whew! You sure you didn't kill him, Jerry?"

"No, Reuben. I had no interest in ending his life. I just didn't want this wildly self-assured son of a bitch around anymore, for the good of the firm. Can you blame me?"

"From all I've heard, I think not. You didn't exactly execute— I mean, fire—him without real cause."

After carelessly using the word "execute," Reuben made a quick exit as soon as decency allowed. Afterward, he thought that after his sessions with Townley, Lander, and Gilbert, they and Detective Muldoon could handle the Joyner case. He had a hunch he would be busy enough with the Courtland murder, which seemed more significant to the future well-being of the firm than the death of a horny, less-than-stellar associate with a giant ego and an unrealistic view of his own abilities.

Fourteen

DARCY WATSON

When Reuben returned to his own office, there was a message from Bautista.

"I was calling to tell you that we've found a copy of the 1938 *Collier's* story by Gere Dexter. It matches the underlined passage in those galley proofs we picked up at Marina's apartment pretty closely."

"Great work, Luis," Reuben said enthusiastically. "But where does that leave us?"

"I decided we'd better see Ms. Watson. See what she knows, if anything. I had to struggle like hell to get her address and phone number out of the Gramercy House people, but I finally did. She lives outside Philadelphia but comes to New York often. In fact, I got hold of her just before she left to get the train to the City. She's staying at something called the Cygnus Club. Do you know it?"

"Lord, yes. It's an old-line women's club. Cynthia's a member and I get dragged there every so often."

"Good. Maybe you can protect me. I'm meeting Ms. Watson there at eight thirty tomorrow morning. You up for it?"

"As long as she doesn't want to read to us from one of her dreadful novels."

Late that afternoon, Bautista called Reuben again.

"I'm afraid you've been disinvited to our party tomorrow morning."

"What do you mean?"

"Ms. Watson just called to check to make sure she would be seeing me alone. She didn't mention you specifically, but said she didn't want to deal with any 'outsiders.'"

"I suspect she had a little talk with my great friend John Sommers."

"That's what I think, too," Bautista said. "So I guess I'll be on my own. Is there anything you can tell me about her?"

"I've already passed on to you what Cynthia told me, that the Cygnus Club seems to be her home away from home. Nobody seems to know much about her personal life. Never married, Cynthia thinks. I've seen a couple of gossip-column references to her being with Sommers at some social event or another. But that's about all I can tell you."

"Maybe I should try to read one of her books."

"Spare yourself that, Luis. God knows I've never read one, but she's supposed to be 'uplifting,' with novels upholding 'family values.'"

"I guess I can skip them."

"She also wears *salwar kameezes*," Reuben said mischievously.

"What?"

Reuben took delight in explaining his recently acquired knowledge about Indian fashion and then wished Luis good luck. "Call me when you're finished with her. I'll be curious to hear what she has to say."

Bautista was not put at ease by his fellow Latino doorman at the Cygnus Club. But having gained admission, he was directed to a large reception room that looked like the lobby of a Caribbean resort with its light pink walls, pastel-covered furniture, and tall rubber plants in each corner.

Alone in the room at the early hour, he heard the elevator out in the corridor open and heard Ms. Watson approach even before he saw her. When he did, he immediately understood what a *kameeze*—in this case a bright yellow one—and a *salwar*—bright green—were. In fact, the tall woman, with her upswept black hair, looked like a giant sunflower.

"Mr. Bautista?" she inquired as she approached and shook hands. "Good morning. As I told you on the telephone, I suspect this little meeting is a waste of your time as well as mine, but of course I'll help you in any way I can.

"I should also warn you though that I must leave here not later than nine thirty. I have a class—my creative writing class—at Hunter College at ten."

"I'm sure we can meet your schedule," Luis said as the two sat down in chairs facing each other. Taking out his notebook, he asked her if she was familiar with the Marina Courtland case.

"Of course, but only indirectly through her father. You undoubtedly already know that I'm currently seeing him. Needless to say, the death of his daughter has preoccupied him of late. The poor man.

"To answer your question, I didn't happen to be present

when the evil deed occurred," she said sarcastically. She shifted her weight impatiently and stroked her upswept hair.

"Did you ever discuss her with Mr. Sommers?"

"Probably, but I don't recall a specific conversation. I was curious about her after she introduced me to her father. One day when we were both at Gramercy House."

"Did you have any impression of her?"

"Yes, I did. She worked with me and John on my latest book, although only in a junior capacity. John's my real editor and always has been."

"Did you talk to Mr. Sommers yesterday, after we first talked?"

"Yes. I was curious to know what was going on and why you wanted to see me."

"What did he say?"

"That you were searching under every rock, and that I was probably one of them. One of the rocks."

"Did Mr. Sommers ever mention an email that he had received from Miss Courtland? An email alleging that a passage from your recent novel was lifted from an old magazine story?"

"Oh, is she the one?! I didn't make the connection. John told me somebody in the office had made such a ridiculous charge but didn't mention any name. He said he would take care of the person, I assume by firing him or her. I took it for granted that he'd done so and didn't think any more about it. The whole thing was absurd."

"So Miss Courtland's charge was baseless?"

"Absolutely."

"If I told you we have a copy of the *Collier's* story she referred to, would that change your answer?"

"No, it wouldn't. If there's some sort of chance literary coincidence here, so be it. That happens all the time."

"Even when there's a word-for-word similarity?"

"Mr. Bautista, I think we can end this rude interrogation right here. I'm not going to listen to you repeat libels by a young junior editor, especially one that, in my case, may have been jealous for entirely personal reasons." She started to stand up.

"As you please, Ms. Watson. But one more question, if I may. Where were you the night of April twenty-seventh?"

"At my home in Ardmore, Pennsylvania. Except for my weekly trips to New York to teach, and occasionally to see John or Dan, I'm always in Ardmore. Unless I'm out on a book tour, which I haven't been since my previous novel came out."

"Can anyone verify that you were in Ardmore that evening?"

"I doubt it very much. I'm a very private person and see almost no one when I'm at home. I *write*, not socialize. So I guess you'll just have to take my word for it."

"As you say, Ms. Watson."

Darcy Watson left the room and the Club without speaking any further.

Fifteen

BEN GILBERT

Against his own counsel of non-interference, Reuben did finally call Bautista on Monday of the next week.

"You fellows on vacation?" he asked.

"Negative. Just being methodical, thanks very much."

"I'm sorry, Luis. I'm sure you are. It's just that curiosity got the better of me."

"We've been working like hell. The commissioner's on our back and the halitosis I smell might even mean someone higher up is breathing down my neck. Unfortunately, the work we've been doing has led us to exclude some possibilities rather than to include any new ones."

Bautista went on to explain that he and his colleagues had found the young fortune hunter that Marina Courtland had rejected a couple of years before. He was now attending the Harvard Business School and appeared to have an airtight alibi for the night of her murder: participating in a reading group of fellow students discussing a new book on the Boston Strangler.

"Slight irony there, I should say," Reuben interrupted.

"Yeah. Can you believe it? But all eight guys participating swear he was there. The other thing we're doing, Reuben, we're going through her address book and her cell phone and calling every number. And we're examining every piece of paper we took away from her office and her apartment. So far we've come up dry, but we've got a long ways to go. But stand by, Reuben, we'll get there."

"I hope so. I've got to get Dan Courtland off my back. He can't fire you but he can fire my law firm."

"Keep it cool, Reuben, I'll write if I get work."

"I've found work, I think," Luis told Reuben in an early after-noon phone conversation less than forty-eight hours later. "I think we've solved at least one mystery."

"What's that?" Reuben asked eagerly.

"Can I come over?"

"Since you're not going to tell me now, what choice do I have? Hurry up."

Bautista related the new developments when he arrived. It seems that first thing that morning, a young man named Ben Gilbert had shown up at the Nineteenth Precinct on East Sixty-Seventh Street. When he told the desk officer in charge that he had been a friend of Marina Courtland, he was hustled off to the headquarters of Detective Borough Manhattan on Twenty-First Street. Luis summarized his story:

Gilbert was a medical resident in pediatrics at Cornell-New York Hospital. With his uncertain schedule and demanding hours at the hospital, he had found little time for dating, so a friend suggested he try an Internet service called Meet.com. The friend said he could warn potential dates about his haphazard schedule, and only those who were willing to put up with it would respond.

He had gone out with several girls contacted through Meet.com, with varying results. He had become especially attracted to a young woman named Hallie Miller, whom he described as being a junior editor in a publishing house, though he didn't know which one. She was terrific, and sympathetic to the professional demands on his time and uncomplaining about frequent changes in their dating schedule. This had often meant rendezvous at sometimes less than satisfactory late-night restaurants.

At some point, he decided that he was really interested in Miller and told her as much. Her response was to suggest that the two have dinner—during normal hours. They did, and it was over this meal that she confided that she was not Hallie Miller but Marina Courtland.

"And why did this fellow say she had done such a thing—using an assumed name?" Reuben interrupted.

"She explained to Gilbert that she'd had a bitter experience with a party who was after her money. You remember we were told about that. She thought she could find someone on Meet.com without money being a factor, and then come clean if the situation developed."

"Extraordinary, but that fits with what we've been thinking."

"I agree."

"So what happened to this Gilbert fellow?"

"As he tells it, the money angle drove him away. He wasn't ready to take on a billionaire's daughter, at least not one whose father had views like those of old man Courtland. Gilbert's been a poor scholarship student all along and didn't think he'd fit in with the Courtlands."

"He wasn't interested in being set up for life?"

"No. He didn't seem like that type of guy at all."

"So there are young people who aren't totally greedy, out for the buck? Thank God, if that's true."

"In his case, it seems to be."

"Didn't he have any suspicion that she was using a different name?"

"No, apparently not. He found it odd that she never asked him to her apartment, but thought that she probably had a roommate she didn't want to tell him about. So their more intimate moments were in his tiny studio apartment on York Avenue, near the hospital. Only after the truth came out did he attach any significance to the fact that she never paid with a credit card when it was her turn to pay. She always had plenty of cash with her."

"What persuaded this fellow to come to the police?" Reuben asked.

"He said he'd been reading about the murder in the papers and thought her murderer might be someone she'd met on the Internet."

"A sort of virtual Mr. Goodbar."

"Exactly."

"Not Mr. Gilbert?" Reuben asked.

"Don't think so."

"What do we know about him?"

"He gave me his personal ID and password for the Meet.com website."

"Is that *M-E-E-T* or *M-E-A-T*?"

"Meet.com. *M-E-E-T*, Reuben, for heaven's sake. Anyway he gave me the info to get into his profile on the site."

"So what did you learn?"

"He's twenty-seven. Red hair, one hundred eighty-five pounds, six feet even. Cornell College and Medical School. Likes intelligent, amusing girls, preferably pretty ones."

"How original."

"Wants to get married but not until he finishes his residency. Wants three children."

"Anything else?" Reuben asked.

"Oh yes. Doesn't smoke, drinks moderately. Didn't answer the question about his income—probably because it's less than zero."

"Luis, do you realize, assuming Mr. Gilbert is telling the truth, that with a few clicks on the Internet, you got more information than a squad of detectives could have discovered in a week, maybe a month, maybe never?"

"Yeah, I thought about that. There's more, too. Once Gilbert put his profile on the site, girls could respond. Hallie Miller did, so her profile is available, too. And there is a record of the emails between Gilbert and her."

"Any surprises?"

"No, there are about half a dozen messages, but all about arranging to get together."

"What about her profile?"

"I brought a copy with me. If HallieNYC, as she calls herself, is telling the truth, it's pretty revealing." Bautista pulled several pages from a manila envelope he was carrying and handed them to Reuben. "Here, read it for yourself."

Reuben did so.

HallieNYC

26-year-old woman   [No picture]
New York, New York
seeking men 26–45
within New York City

About me and what I'm looking for:
I've been in New York City for two years, but I feel like a native. I'm more comfortable here than I ever was in the Midwest, where I grew up. I guess I'm a Blue-Stater at heart.

I work as a junior editor at a small publishing house and enjoy it very much. I love everything about the literary life, though my reading preferences are by no means confined to high-brow stuff; murder mysteries are definitely on my agenda. For example, I'm crazy for anything written by Julian Barnes, including the detective novels he wrote under the name Dan Kavanagh. My tastes are not exclusively literary, however. A good play, an exciting jazz concert, or a dance performance can get me out of my easy chair. And so will a good meal (and some good wine to go with it).

I'm looking for someone who is bright, down-to-earth, funny—even sarcastic—and honest, who can share the fun of the absurdities of Manhattan. He also should be kind and compassionate. Not a Wall Street or financial type interested only in money, conspicuous consumption, and getting ahead. I'm sorry to say he shouldn't be bald, either. He should be open-minded and good at communicating. With or without words.

I want someone to spend good times with and, if something more serious develops, well, great!

I consider myself above-average looking but I haven't included a picture here because I can't see basing a relationship on looks alone (particularly looks hyped-up in a doctored photograph).

More About Me:
Relationship: Never married
Have kids: None
Want kids: Someday
Ethnicity: White/Caucasian

Body type: Slender
Height: 5′6″
Hair: Black
Eyes: Hazel
Best Feature: Legs
Body art: Small figure, lower abdomen (college mistake)
Religion: [No answer]
Smoke: Occasionally
Drink: Social drinker
Sports: Tennis, swimming, walking, hiking
Exercise: 2 times a week
Education: BA
Income: [No answer]
Languages: English, French
Politics: Liberal to radical
Likes: Reading, discussing books, jazz (all kinds), travel
      (including weekends), wine tastings, dining
Dislikes: Crude pornography, flirting, money talk, words
      and phrases like "freebie," "hang-ups," "hooking up,"
      "issues," "cyberspace," and "pushing back"

About the date I want:
Hair: Any color (but not bald, as I said)
Eyes: Any color
Height: 5′7″ on up
Body type: Doesn't matter; but good shape a must
Ethnicity: Prefer white/Caucasian, but will consider others
Religion: Any or none, as long as not rigid or fanatical
Education: At least a BA
Occupation: Anything not boring
Income: Irrelevant, but not a sponge

Smoke: OK
Drink: Moderate drinking OK
Have kids: No
Want kids: Wait and see

Luis waited while Reuben read the entire document.

"Interesting," Reuben remarked when he'd finished, returning the printout to the detective. "Doesn't quite accord with Dan Courtland's view of his daughter—the little tattoo, wine tasting, drinking, smoking. Communicating 'with and without words.' That's a good one. And 'liberal to radical' politics. Dan would especially like that. I'm not terribly surprised, though."

Reuben asked whether it was usual to have a picture with these "so-called profiles."

"Yes, I'm told there's nearly always at least a selfie."

"Hmm. I suspect she didn't submit hers because she was afraid someone might identify her as Marina Courtland."

"That's my guess, too."

"Now the sixty-four-dollar question, Luis—who else contacted HallieNYC besides Mr. Gilbert?"

"We don't have any idea. The only reason we know as much as we do, and have that profile you just read, is because we had access to Gilbert's account. She was just one of the people *he* contacted. But to know who else Hallie/Marina was in touch with, we'd have to know her password to get into her file."

"It sure as hell isn't like mixer dances," Reuben muttered. "Can't this Meet.com outfit give you the information?"

"Thought of that. Unfortunately, it's based in Bermuda."

"Damn. Isn't there any other way?"

"Maybe. Let me explain. My IT guy can get to Meet.com on the computer and insert Marina Courtland's ID—HallieNYC.

Then it asks for a password, which is what we don't have. But it also has a line to click 'Forgot your password?' When you do that the program asks for your birth date—we have that—and another fail-safe question selected earlier by the user, in this case 'What was the name of your first pet?' If we had that, we could get into Marina's data and find out who she was contacting—or was contacted by."

"Name of her first pet? That's ridiculous."

"Most of the test questions are ridiculous—name of your pet, name of your first boyfriend, mother's maiden name, et cetera. The idea is to pick some obscure fact that only the user, in this case Marina, would know. You pick the question and give the answer when you sign up. Then, if you forget your password, they ask you the question and if you give the right answer, they email you your password or instruct you how to get a new one."

"Dan Courtland's the only one who's likely to know the answer to that silly question. And I have a hunch that's a long shot. Should I call him?"

"No harm done."

"Come on, let's go upstairs." They went to Reuben's study and he dialed Daniel's number. His secretary, Grace Wrightson, said that her boss was at the Indianapolis Speedway, but could be reached on his cell. This worked, though the background noise at the Speedway garage was very loud. Reuben put him on speakerphone so that Luis could hear. He also quickly told Daniel that the detective was in on the conversation before he could make a slighting remark about the police.

"I assume, Officer Bautista, the news is still the same—that is, that there's no news," Courtland said. "Almost three weeks—*three weeks!*—after my daughter's murder."

"We may have a break, sir," Luis said.

"What is it?" Daniel shouted into the phone.

"It depends on a small bit of information that I hope you can provide us with. What was the name of Marina's first pet?"

"What? Are you out of your mind? Reuben, what's going on there?"

Reuben managed to calm Daniel down, and paraphrased the explanation Luis had just given him. He told Daniel that "it was too complicated to go into detail," but the police needed to get into one of Marina's computer files and knowing the name of her first pet was necessary to accomplish that.

"I don't have any idea. I don't even remember what her first pet was, or how old she was when she got it. She must have had two dozen pets over the years—dogs, cats, a pony, a turtle, even a snake at one point."

"Did Marina perhaps have a nanny who might remember?" Reuben asked.

"Yes. Maureen. But she went back to Ireland, and I understand she died there a couple years ago."

Reuben and Luis looked at each other and shrugged.

"I guess that's that," Reuben said. "But, Dan, if you can think of anyone—anyone at all—who might know, please get in touch with them and ask them."

"Are you going to tell me what this is all about?"

"Putting it simply," Reuben said, "she may have been communicating online with the person who killed her."

"Oh."

"We'll be in touch," Reuben said.

"I sure hope so."

Cynthia came in from shopping at this point and Reuben asked her to join Luis and him in the study.

"I think it's time for a drink," Reuben said.

"Sure," Luis replied. "I'm off-duty for the day, except for my time with the twins. So make it a double Scotch and water."

The two men reviewed the bidding for Cynthia over their drinks. They were pleased that Ben Gilbert had come forward and probably solved the two-name puzzle, but they realized they were no closer to solving the bigger poser: the identity of Marina Courtland's killer. They also explained the roadblock to accessing HallieNYC's account at Meet.com.

"You boys are slipping," Cynthia said. "What about Gino Facini? Don't you think he might know the name of his half-sister's first pet?"

"Good heavens, of course," Reuben said a bit sheepishly. "I've even got his cell number." Without another word, he rushed back to his study, retrieved Gino's number, and called it. Unfortunately, he got voicemail, rather than the young actor himself. Reuben, in turn, asked Gino to call him as soon as possible and then reported back his lack of success to Cynthia and Luis.

"Well, let's hope he calls and can answer the pet question," Cynthia said.

"I'll drink to that," her husband added.

Sixteen

PASSWORD

Gino Facini called shortly after eleven that evening. Reuben was still up and took the call, explaining to Gino the information needed and why.

"She was screwing around with that Internet dating crap?" Gino asked. "She probably was killed by one of the nuts who go in for that stuff."

Reuben asked the question about her first pet.

"How should I remember that? I was five years older than she was, and she probably had her first pet when she was maybe three and I was eight. She had real crazy names for all the animals she had while we were growing up—Bruno and Carlotta. Much later Marlon—after you know who. She even had a God period—not surprising, given her father—and called a spaniel she had Francis, after Saint Francis. Not to mention Beelzebub, a big black Labrador."

"But what about the very first one? Try hard, Gino," Reuben encouraged.

"Okay, it's coming back to me. The first one I remember was a young kitten named Marian. I teased her about it because the cat was a boy and we had a neighbor, a girl, named Marian. But she was stubborn, as always, even at that age, and insisted on the name. Was that her first pet? I think so. It was the first one I remember, anyway."

Marian. What an unlikely name. But it was worth a try. Reuben called Luis, who said he'd be over first thing the next morning.

"Let's hope we've got it," he said.

Thursday morning, the two men did not wait to have coffee before going straight to Reuben's computer.

"I would have tried this out last night, but I wasn't entirely sure how you go about it," Reuben said. Seated at the keyboard of his PC, with Bautista sitting beside him, he asked for the exact name of the site they wanted.

"Meet.com."

"With an '*E-E*,' you told me. Here goes." He typed in the name and an opening screen came up, asking for the user's ID. Reuben typed in *HallieNYC*. Then clicked to indicate he had forgotten her password and entered her birth date and *Marian* in response to the pet-name question. They waited anxiously as the screen disappeared, but anxiety changed to disappointment when an error message reading INCORRECT RESPONSE TO TEST QUESTION came up.

"Damn!" Reuben exploded. "What did we do wrong?"

"I don't think anything. Try it again."

Reuben did so, very carefully, but the error message came up again.

Cynthia, passing by at that moment, stuck her head in the door of the study and asked how it was going.

"Badly, very badly," her husband told her. He explained how the word *Marian* had been rejected as an answer to the site's test question.

Cynthia thought about this and then said, "You know, there are two ways of spelling *Marian*—with an *A* or with an *O*."

Reuben and Luis looked at each other. Hurriedly they tried again, answering *Marion* to the test question. The message that came on the screen told them that a temporary password was being sent in an email message to Hallie's account.

"We're getting there!" Reuben shouted as he retrieved the password, inserted it along with Hallie's ID, and within seconds reached Meet.com's home page for members.

"Cynthia, you're a genius!" he called out to his wife.

"Yes, I've often been told that," Cynthia said, laughing.

Luis got up and shook her hand vigorously and gave her big kisses on both cheeks. "It's all downhill from here," he said.

"Not so fast, Luis," Reuben said. "We've got some more digging to do."

"I'd love to join you boys, but I have a staff meeting at the Foundation this morning, so I'll have to leave you to your fun."

"We'll keep you posted," Luis told her.

"Let's see what we have to do now," Reuben said, as he read the directions on the screen. After some trial and error they found that they could get to the individual profiles of all the men who had communicated with "Hallie." There were eight, including Ben Gilbert. All had pictures attached except one; none was recognized by either Reuben or Luis. They scanned each of the files that contained email correspondence between Hallie and the proprietor of that file. Ben Gilbert's confirmed the details he had related to the police. Four others had clicked HELLO—the way of making initial contact on Meet.com. Marina, presumably after reviewing their profiles, had not answered them. That left three, which they combed through more carefully.

In the first email file, there were six messages, but they ended with a kiss-off from the male party. "I've enjoyed our virtual flirtation," he wrote, "but I don't think you and I are a fit. Too bad, but thanks anyway. Pampered Prince."

The second was eight messages long, with a sign off from Hallie. "I've really enjoyed our fencing—much fun—but I have to tell you I'm now pretty much involved with somebody else. Maybe later? HallieNYC."

That left the last file, from Waggerson444, the file without a picture. It was the longest of the group, and Reuben and Luis scrolled through it quickly. Two entries, both dated April 26, the day before Marina was murdered, caught their eye.

> To: Waggerson444
> From: HallieNYC
> Date: April 26 0800
>
>
> Before we go off for the weekend—which I'm really looking forward to a lot, I'd like to have a quiet Friday-night dinner with you. How about a place up near me called Quatorze, on 79th and 2nd? Like 8 o'clock? Then we can have dinner and get that plane for Jamaica at eleven. OK? H.
>
> To: HallieNYC
> From: Waggerson444
> Date: April 26 1005
>
>
> Perfect. I'm not flying this time, but driving—from Boston tomorrow. (Have to go to a godforsaken spot in Pennsylvania next week and driving there is easier than

flying. Besides, it will be easier having a car at the airport when we get back Sunday, as it's usually a mess at JFK on summer Sundays, as you probably know.) I'll park near the restaurant tomorrow night.

They tell me you're not supposed to use capital letters in email messages BUT I CAN'T WAIT! See you at Quatorze Bis (why couldn't you pick a restaurant easier to spell?) tomorrow at 8. With bags packed AND READY TO GO! T.

Their curiosity piqued, they started reading the file from the beginning.

To: HallieNYC
From: Waggerson444
Date: March 6 0955

I like your profile—and the conclusion of the Meet.com computer that we are "89% compatible." Should we find out about the missing 11%?

I also agree with you about no picture, as you will see from my profile. This means you take a gamble, and so do I, if we get together. Maybe I'm one of the seven dwarfs and you are Daisy Duck. But should we chance it? Tom

To: Waggerson444
From: HallieNYC
Date: March 7 2033

I'll gamble. Call me on my cell at 917-445-7821. Hallie

To: Waggerson444
From: HallieNYC
Date: March 13 1122

Tom, I enjoyed last night a lot. More like 95% than 89%.
Let's do it again! And you don't look at all like one of the
seven dwarfs. Hallie

To: HallieNYC
From: Waggerson444
Date: March 13 0947

I'm going to be stuck in Boston for a few days. However, I
should be back in NYC on Thursday, the 22nd. Dinner? Tom
    P.S.—And you don't look like Daisy Duck.

To: Waggerson444
From: Hallie NYC
Date: March 17 2001

Sounds good to me. Same place as last time? 8 o'clock?
Hallie

To: HallieNYC
From: Waggerson444
Date: March 19 1001
Yes! Tom

To: Waggerson444
From: HallieNYC
Date: March 23 1122

After last night I think we're at 98%. Maybe even 99. Very satisfying, as I hope it was for you. And I like that suite/hotel—or sweet hotel?—where you stay. Cute and comfortable. Hallie

To: HallieNYC
From: Waggerson444
Date: March 28 0935

Sorry I missed your call last night. I had my cell turned off when I went to the theater and figured it was too late to call you by the time I got home. Tom

To: Waggerson444
From: HallieNYC
Date: March 28 2008

No problem. I was just calling to see when we can meet up again. I miss you.

To: Waggerson444
From: HallieNYC
Date: April 4 1050

Sorry about last night, which must have been about 80% for you. I've been having a rather nasty quarrel that involves a guy at work, my father, and his girlfriend. Don't ask. I'm sure my anxiety came through. Forgive me? Love, Hallie

To: HallieNYC

From: Waggerson444
Date: April 5 1120

Forgiven. It was more like 90% anyway. Tom

To: Waggerson444
From: HallieNYC
Date: April 9 1918

Sorry you're tied up in Boston this week. Have you finished the Julian Barnes stories I gave you? He's over here
in the States doing a book tour and I saw him on TV last
night. Will it make you jealous if I say I fell in love with
him? Love (to you, too), Hallie

To: HallieNYC
From: Waggerson444
Date: April 17 0958

I've read a couple of the stories. He's clever, no question
about it.
    Thursday, the usual? Love, Tom

To: Waggerson444
From: HallieNYC
Date: April 17 2049

How about a change of venue? I haven't been to Boston in
ages. Would be great to be there with you.
    Love, Hallie

To: HallieNYC
From: Waggerson444
Date: April 18 0949

Why not? Only problem is I really get sucked into late hours, entertaining potential investors, etc. But let's talk about it and see if we can work something out. Love, Tom

"True love, you think?" Reuben asked Luis.

"Maybe. But I'll bet he's married."

"Why?"

"He doesn't want her in Boston, if that's really where he lives."

"Let's try his profile," Reuben said. "See what we can find there."

They did so.

Waggerson444

45-year-old man   [No picture]
Boston/New York
seeking women 25–45
Boston/New York

About me and what I'm looking for:
I live in Boston, but I commute to New York City so much I feel like a resident there. I'm a private investor who has been lucky with a variety of investments, including some technology ones that I got out of before the high-tech collapse. I've been pretty much of a loner because of the

demands of my work; my marriage went down the tubes because of that.

Now I'm looking to kick back and enjoy myself more. I want to break out and meet someone I do *not* have to talk business with. I need to meet someone who is fun and intelligent and, above all, relaxed and non-obsessive. Good looks a plus, needless to say.

My name is Tom, by the way.

More About Me:
Relationship: Divorced
Have kids: None
Want kids: Doubt it
Ethnicity: White/Caucasian
Body type: Muscular
Height: 6′2″
Hair: Brown
Eyes: Blue
Best Feature: Haven't any idea; chest maybe
Body art: Absolutely none
Religion: Agnostic
Smoke: No
Drink: Social drinker
Sports: Swimming, diving, tennis
Exercise: 3 times a week
Education: BA, MBA
Income: [No answer]
Languages: English
Politics: Middle-of-the-road
Likes: Theatre, concerts, travel, gourmet meals
Dislikes: Airheads, chatterboxes

About the date I want:

Hair: Any color

Eyes: Any color

Height: 5′5″ on up

Body type: Slim and curvy

Ethnicity: White/Caucasian

Religion: Not important to me

Education: At least a BA

Occupation: Something different than mine

Income: Not a factor

Smoke: OK

Drink: Social drinking OK

Have kids: No

Want kids: No

"All right, who is he?" Bautista asked when they had finished.

"Not a clue," said Reuben. "Divorced, white, Boston private investor. Forty-five years old. Doesn't fit anyone I know."

"Of course, every one of those 'facts' you just reeled off could be lies. I'm told that many if not most of the people that use these matching services lie about themselves. But let's give it a try."

"What are you doing?" Reuben asked.

"Calling directory assistance in Boston. To see if there's a Thomas Waggerson listed."

The answer was no.

"Google! That's it!" Reuben exclaimed, turning again to the computer. But once Google was keyed up, the only Thomas Waggerson referred to had died in 1779.

"Looks like a dead end," Bautista said. "He has a cell phone, so I'll have the boys check that out—see if there's a number for Mr. Waggerson. Since he also had a vehicle they can check that out, too.

"If those leads don't pan out—and I'm afraid I'm pessimistic since 'Tom Waggerson' may be as fictional as 'Hallie Miller'—where does that leave us? Right where we started?" Reuben asked.

"Not quite. It appears that he and Hallie met up at a restaurant called Quatorze Bis the night she was killed. What are you doing for dinner tomorrow night?"

"I've been there. Nice place. I'd be pleased to dine there with you, Detective."

As for dining that night, Reuben had agreed to accompany Cynthia to the Cygnus Club to hear a young downtown artist, Jacobo Casciano, deliver a lecture, accompanied by slides, on his paintings and drawings, followed by dinner.

"Uplift, my dear, that's what the Cygnus Club is all about," Cynthia had told him. "It won't do you any harm."

"All right. As long as we get there early enough for me to order a martini before the talk begins."

They did indeed arrive early, and were pleasantly surprised at Casciano's articulate and witty talk on his art. Dinner was pedestrian as usual, at least by Reuben's lights, but the couple did find an extraordinary bargain on the Club's wine list—a 2000 Saint-Émilion, albeit a *cru bourgeois*—that tempered Reuben's usual Cygnus Club impatience.

After dinner, as they were strolling toward the entrance, they passed a display case containing photographs of the Club's annual "revels," a pre-Lenten celebration in which the members performed skits, sang nonsense songs, and generally carried on in an outrageously silly fashion. Reuben had accompanied Cynthia to one such annual event and vowed never to do it again. A vow he had kept during her thirty years of membership in the Club.

Stopping to look over the display, Reuben asked, "Who the hell is that?" pointing to a picture of a formidably large woman, in drag—tails, a cape, a top hat, and a fake mustache—pretending to choke a smaller and seemingly terrified victim.

Cynthia took a closer look. "Oh my," she exclaimed. "Even in that ridiculous outfit and pose, there's no mistaking her. It's Darcy Watson."

"Hmm. Sorry Luis didn't see that when he was here earlier today. Isn't it just possible that life followed art?"

"Don't be ridiculous, Reuben."

"I'm not. All I'm saying is that that woman could be Marina Courtland's murderer and, let's face it, she had a motive to kill her."

"It's time we went home," Cynthia said. "Just let me do one thing first."

"Where are you going?"

"Just wait here."

Reuben continued to gaze at the revels pictures until Cynthia returned.

"I have a little surprise for you, dear. On a hunch, I checked at the office to see if by chance Darcy Watson stayed here at the Club the night of April twenty-seventh. And the fact is she did."

"Good God."

Seventeen

QUATORZE

"Life is getting complicated," Reuben told Luis when he called him Friday morning.

"What do you mean?"

Reuben passed along the information that Darcy Watson had been in New York the night of the murder, contrary to what she had told Luis.

"Could she possibly have done it?" Reuben asked. He told Bautista about the pirate picture. "I've never seen her, but from that picture it sure looked as if she'd be capable of choking someone to death without any difficulty."

"I have seen her," Luis replied. "And I don't have any doubt about that. She's one big woman under all those silk clothes. With big hands, I remember."

"Well, think about it. Meanwhile, I'll see you tonight."

As planned, the two men met for dinner at Quatorze Bis on East Seventy-Ninth Street. Reuben had been there before—he was enough of a local to know it as simply *Quatorze*—but he was not acquainted with the staff.

"It's a good, solid bistro-type place," he told Luis. He gestured to the walls, which were lined with book jackets of works from authors both well-known and less known. All were customers and mostly denizens of the neighborhood. The choices ranged from bestsellers to a doctor's diet book.

"Even if we don't discover anything, we'll have a decent meal," Reuben added.

They had deliberately made their reservation for nine thirty, on the theory that the staff would be better able to talk to them at a later, less busy hour.

The maître d' turned out to be a friendly fellow named Gary. He did not take umbrage when they rejected a small banquette next to other diners and asked for a table instead.

"We have some business to transact," Luis told him.

"Sure. No problem." Gary seated them at a table for four, and removed two place settings without complaint. Reuben noted with amusement that they were seated under the book jacket for a recent gory murder mystery.

He asked for a martini, and Luis, technically on duty, settled for a glass of the house Chardonnay.

"Happy anniversary," Luis said, when the drinks arrived.

"What do you mean?"

"Marina Courtland was killed just two weeks ago tonight."

"Oh," Reuben said, raising his glass. Then he asked Luis if he had had any further thoughts about Darcy Watson.

"Just one," he said. "If she was lying about her whereabouts that night, maybe John Sommers was, too. Maybe they acted together."

"Interesting idea. That hadn't occurred to me."

"I've got a detective friend out in Suffolk County. I'm going to get him to check on Sommers's alibi—his story that he had dinner out there on the fatal night. Probably should have done it before this."

Both he and Reuben ordered oysters—Malpeques—and attacked them enthusiastically.

"Damn good," Reuben observed.

They then settled into portions of *blanquette de veau*, a favorite of Reuben's, who pronounced it more than satisfactory. By the time they had finished, the restaurant, full to capacity when they had arrived, was almost empty.

"You know, Luis, it's the damndest thing," Reuben said, looking around. "I've always been told that everyone in Los Angeles, or at least Hollywood, eats early. People want others to think that they're involved in shooting a movie at sunrise the next day. Now the same thing's happening in New York. Not just at this place, but every restaurant Cynthia and I go to. What's going on? Can you explain it?"

"Terrorism," Luis replied.

"Oh, for heaven's sake. What on earth does terrorism have to do with people eating early?"

"I was kidding, Reuben. But terrorism, or fear of terrorism, is now the all-purpose excuse for everything. For instance: My wife left me? Traumatized by fear of ISIS. Can't get it up? Spooked by ISIS. Haven't you noticed? It's the universal alibi."

"Let's get back to the business at hand," Reuben said, with a sigh. "I'm reasonably sure terrorists didn't have anything to do with our problem."

"That's about all we're sure of," Bautista replied. He called over Gary, the maître d', and explained that he was in the midst of a criminal investigation. He produced a print of the photograph from Hallie Miller's fake driver's license. "Do you know this girl?" the detective asked, discreetly handing the print over.

Gary looked at the photo and said, "Sure, I know her."

"Name?"

"Hallie Miller. One of our regular customers."

"What can you tell us about her?"

"I think she lives right around the corner. She comes in about once a week. Some of the waiters and I know her pretty well. We kid around a lot. She's usually here alone and sits at the table on the end in the back, reading a manuscript or galleys while she eats. We tease her all the time about not having a boyfriend and why she doesn't get married."

"Did your teasing get a reaction?" Reuben asked.

"She always says she has all the time in the world to get married, and we'd be the first to know when she finds someone."

"Has she been here lately?" Bautista asked.

"Come to think of it, I haven't seen her in a while. Ten days maybe?"

"How about two weeks ago tonight?" Bautista prompted.

"That could be. Yeah, you're right. It was very odd, that day, because she came here twice. Something she'd never done before."

Bautista and Frost exchanged glances.

"You mean she had both lunch and dinner here?" Reuben asked.

"Yes."

"Very strange. I realize your food is pretty good, sir, but twice in one day is certainly out of the ordinary," Reuben observed.

"And you knew her by the name Hallie Miller?" Bautista asked.

"That's what I said."

"No other name?"

"No." Gary looked puzzled. "What are you getting at?"

"We have reason to believe that Hallie Miller and Marina Courtland, the woman—"

"Oh my God! The billionaire's daughter they found murdered over by the river?"

"Correct."

"Jesus, one of our waiters saw her picture in the paper and said she looked like Hallie. We had an argument about it. As I recall, the newspaper shot was her college graduation picture. It looked something like Hallie, but I was sure it wasn't. But now you're telling me that Hallie was murdered?"

"Yes. And on the very night you last saw her here. So help us with any detail you can recall about that lunch or that dinner. Let's start with the lunch. Was she alone?" Bautista pressed.

"No, she wasn't. And she wasn't at dinner, either. Both times she had a guy with her—a different one each time. I guess that's why I remember the day, because she almost always ate by herself, as I told you."

"Tell me about the fellow at lunch."

"I don't remember too much about him. He was pretty trim, but much older. Could have been old enough to be her father."

"Ever meet her father?"

"No, not that I'm aware of."

"What about the one at night?" Bautista asked.

"He was much younger, but still older than Hallie—Marina. I'd never seen him before, either."

Gary got up to say good night to the last dinner guests. When he returned, he asked if Bautista and Frost wanted to talk to a couple of the waiters who knew her. Bautista agreed that this was a good idea.

"Let me get them before they go home," Gary said, heading back to the kitchen.

Soon they were a group of five—Gary, Bautista, Frost, and two waiters, Jerrod and Matt—sitting around an empty table, the two waiters in their "after-hours" clothes of T-shirts, jeans, and sneakers. The new arrivals looked as stunned as Gary had when Bautista told them the purpose of his visit.

"I told you that newspaper picture looked like Hallie, Gary!" Matt said.

"You were right, kid. It just seemed too improbable. That Hallie could have been leading a double life. Or that Hallie was wildly rich—she certainly never acted like a richie here."

"She was a great girl," Matt volunteered. "I'm practicing to be a professional drummer when not working at my slave job"—he looked at Gary as he said this (though he was smiling)—"and she was real encouraging when other people thought I was crazy."

"You're right, Matt," Jerrod said. "She was always interested in us and what we were doing. I remember about a year ago, I got a part in an off-off-off Broadway show—really bad production of *The Night of the Iguana*—and she came to see me perform. She was like that. Always cheering you on."

"But, you know, now that you think about it, she kept her distance," Jerrod added. "I never felt I knew anything about her personal life, except that she normally didn't show up here with anyone, until that last day, and that she was a book editor somewhere."

"What about the fellows she was with two weeks ago?" Reuben asked. "If you all were so concerned about her having a boyfriend, you must have been curious about them."

"I wasn't working the lunch shift, so I don't know about the lunch guy," Matt said.

"I worked both shifts," Jerrod added. "At lunch, she sat in her usual place in the back, but with this old fellow she came in with."

"What about him?" Bautista asked. "White hair, brown hair, gray hair?"

"Brown, I guess, what there was of it."

"Fat, thin, stocky, what?"

"Pretty trim. Not fat."

"Glasses?"

"Negative."

"Anything distinctive about him?"

"Not really. He and Hallie seemed very serious. Since he did most of the talking, I assumed he was trying to sell her something. He looked like he might be a salesman."

"Any idea what they were discussing?"

"No, sir, I try not to overhear my customers' conversations. But I could see the talk was intense. They were all business. They also scarcely touched their food."

"How about dinner? Did you serve them again?"

"I saw them when they came in," Matt, who had been silent as Jerrod described the lunch hour, interrupted. "I was working the tables in the back, near the kitchen. It was one of the first nice nights we'd had so she wanted to sit at a table outside on the sidewalk."

"I served them," Jerrod said. "In fact, I started to make a little joke about twice-in-one-day, but Hallie cut me off rather sharply."

"Did they seem affectionate?" Reuben asked.

"Yes, they did. Not all over each other, but, yeah, there was some juice there."

"Did they hold hands?"

"Could be. But I didn't really notice."

"As I told you, I was working the back tables," Matt interrupted again. "At one point Hallie's date came by, on the way to the men's room. I remember thinking he was pretty attractive, but older than she was."

"Was there anything special or odd about them? Anything out of the ordinary, or the way they behaved?" Bautista asked.

Jerrod thought about the question. "I don't think so," he said slowly. "But now that you mention it, they left in a hurry—no dessert, no coffee. Hallie always had dessert. We always told her to watch out, that she'd get fat and unappealing if she kept eating big desserts."

"You're right, Jerrod," Gary chimed in. "It was really busy that night—Friday is our busiest night—and I had it in the back of my mind to go out and say hello to Hallie, and to satisfy my curiosity about who she was with, when I had a chance. But she and her friend paid the check and left before I was able to do that."

"There was one other thing," Jerrod said. "I remember now. A guy came walking down the street and stopped at their table. He and Hallie's date shook hands and he introduced the passerby to her. It was clear the date knew him, but she didn't."

"You sure about that?" Bautista asked.

"Yes, pretty sure. I heard the guy say 'This is Hallie,' but I didn't get his name or the stranger's.

"They chatted for a few minutes and the guy on the street showed them what I guess was his new phone," Jerrod continued. "At least all three of them looked it over like it was something new, laughing about it. Then, just before he walked on, the guy used it to take a picture of Hallie and the guy with her.

"After he left, Hallie and her date had a really animated conversation, I remember. Both of them were gesturing with their arms as they talked. I noticed, because they had been quiet—almost dreamy quiet—before. Then suddenly the fellow with Hallie called for the check and seemed to be in a big hurry. They left as soon as he paid."

"Maybe he had a train to catch?" Reuben suggested.

"Can't help you there," Jerrod said, shrugging. "Maybe. No, wait—he had a set of car keys in his hand when they got up to leave."

"Are you sure about that?"

"Pretty sure, yeah. I figured if they were going off in a car, they weren't going to shack up—pardon me—at her apartment. And I thought that because I saw his keys."

"What time did they leave?"

"I'd say about nine, nine fifteen," Jerrod said.

"What about this stranger who came by her table?" Luis asked.

"I don't really recall much about him."

"Was he tall? Short? Dark hair? Light hair?"

"Medium height maybe, probably Hallie's age or a little older. Conventional-looking. Black hair, I think."

"Anything else you can tell me about him?"

"Afraid not. He didn't leave that much of an impression," Jerrod replied. Luis looked dejected.

"By the way," he asked, having decided he'd reached a dead end regarding the mysterious photographer, "how did she sign her checks when she ate here alone?"

"She always paid cash," Gary said. "Which I guess was necessary if her credit cards were in her real name. But, Jerrod, you said the guy was the one who paid that night."

"Yes."

"With a credit card?" Reuben asked sharply.

"Yes, sir, I'm sure he did."

"And what was his name?"

"I didn't get it."

"What about lunch? Who paid?" Luis asked.

"I'm not sure," Jerrod answered. "All I know was there was a pile of cash on the table to pay the check when they left. No credit card was involved."

"Going back to dinner, with all your curiosity about Hallie's boyfriends, you didn't look at the signer's name, Jerrod?" Reuben had resorted to a cross-examining tone that was unlike him.

"Sorry. We were busy as hell, and they were in a big hurry to leave. I just didn't focus on his name. Wouldn't have meant anything to me anyway."

"How does it work with your credit card receipts?" Bautista asked Gary. "Do you keep them?"

"Yeah, we keep one copy. The boss keeps them for about six months."

"So you could examine the receipts for that night and figure out who was here?"

"At least the ones who paid with a credit card, yes."

"Can we see those?" Bautista asked.

"I'm sure you can. But the owners keep them in the safe and I don't have the combination."

"When will he be here?"

"There are two of them, Mark and Peter. At least one of them is usually here midafternoon, around three or four."

Reuben had a sudden thought, and interrupted. "Did Hallie and her date have a reservation?"

"I'm sure they did. She was a favored customer, but on a Friday night, I'm sure there would have been a reservation."

"How do we check that?" Reuben pressed.

"That would be in the book—I've got it here, right up front," Gary said. He stood up, went to the reception desk and returned with a spiral notebook. He flipped through the pages.

"Here it is, Friday, the twenty-seventh," he said, as he went down the list for that date. "Yeah—got it—eight o'clock, Hallie Miller."

"Not her companion's name?"

"Nope."

"And how about lunch?"

"No reservation at all for that."

"Damn."

Luis sighed. "I guess it's back to the credit cards. I'll be here tomorrow at four o'clock."

"And you'll be here, too?" he asked Gary, who nodded affirmatively.

"And how about you two?"

"I'll be here," Jerrod replied, "but I don't think I can be much help."

"And you, Matt?"

"No, sir, I have a long drumming lesson tomorrow afternoon."

Walking slowly down Seventy-Ninth Street, Reuben and Luis tried to make sense of what they had been told at the restaurant.

"Just what we need, three mystery men," Luis finally concluded. "Hallie's lunch guest, her dinner partner, and the stranger who interrupted her meal."

"I'm only surprised Darcy Watson wasn't there as well," Reuben added with a bitter laugh.

Eighteen

A PREPRANDIAL SHOCK

The Bautistas and the Frosts had arranged to have a weekend dinner the next night. Francesca and Luis, as instructed, arrived at the Frosts' apartment promptly at seven thirty for drinks.

Francesca let out a long sigh as she sat down. She gratefully accepted a glass of Chablis from Reuben. "Don't ever have twins!" she said, then quickly added, "Actually, it's great. Fascinating to see how they're alike, how they're different."

"I assume Rafaela Cynthia is the better behaved of the two?" Cynthia inquired.

"I'm not so sure about that. Manuel Reuben's a very good boy."

"I should hope so," Reuben said. "I would expect so."

Reuben was anxious to get Luis aside, to find out what he had learned at Quatorze that afternoon. Once Cynthia and Francesca began conversing together, he took Luis by the arm and led him to his study. They sat down with their drinks—Reuben with a martini and Luis with a gin and tonic.

"How was the fishing?" Reuben asked. "Hope you had good luck."

"Maybe, maybe not. I'm not sure. There were more than fifty credit card charge slips for the night of April fifteenth. Gary, the guy we met, knew most of the signers and was able to eliminate them. Quite a few chits were signed by women, so those were out, too. In the end, we were left with six that could have been signed by the mysterious stranger."

"Did you recognize any of the names?"

"No. But I put one of my guys to work trying to trace them. We'll just have to wait and see what he comes up with."

"Do you have the list, by the way? I'm curious."

"Affirmative. I brought a copy for you. I figured you'd want to see it. Here it is." He handed Reuben a sheet on which were written six names:

Michael Rosen
Theodore F. Keith
Daniel Rense
Eskill Lander
J. Parke McLeod
Stuart Wiley

Reuben visibly started when he came to Lander's name.

"I do know one of these people," he said hoarsely. "Eskill Lander is one of my partners. He's our senior trust and estates partner. He's the personal attorney for Marina's father. But I'm sure that's merely a weird happenstance."

"Couldn't it be like a 'chance literary coincidence'?"

Reuben shot him a cross look.

"Is he married?" Luis asked.

"Yes, he is," Reuben answered. "Though I'm not sure how happily."

"Ah, so maybe he was having a fling with Miss Courtland?"

"Impossible. Dan Courtland is a major, major client of Chase

& Ward. Nobody at the firm in his right mind would mess with his daughter. You've met the man. With his views, he'd personally stone any adulterer fooling around with her. He'd fire Lander—and our firm—without a second thought."

"But don't forget he thought he was with Hallie Miller," Bautista offered. "That was the name she was known at in the restaurant."

"Oh God, of course you're right."

"No, maybe wrong. Your man Lander must have known Marina Courtland."

"He told me he didn't when we talked about the murder the other day. Said he only dealt with her through correspondence. I hate to say it, but we better take a hard look at him."

"Right. I'm also putting my guys to work on all fifty charge chits, to see if anybody has a recollection of Marina's date or the mysterious stranger with the cell-phone camera. And also to canvas the lunch ones to see if anyone might identify the *first* mysterious stranger who was with Marina."

"That's all well and good, but let's see where we're at," Reuben said. He retrieved a yellow legal pad from his desk. "Let's put down what we know, or don't know," he said. "Or what we *think* we know."

"Number one, Marina had lunch at Quatorze Bis on the day of her death with a mysterious stranger.

"Number two, we think that Lander might be the second mysterious stranger."

"If I can get a picture of Lander, I can see if the guys at the restaurant recognize him," Luis said.

"That's easy. God help us, there are pictures of each of the partners on the firm's website. How the powers that be think that those ugly mugs will attract business I don't know. But I can print a picture for you without any trouble. In fact, I'll do it right now." He clicked to the Chase & Ward website and started his printer.

Luis took the photo when it was finished. "I'm pretty sure the restaurant's open tomorrow. I'll stop by and see if they recognize this guy."

"Number three," Reuben went on, "we think that Marina and Lander were seen by a third mysterious stranger that knew Lander. I wish the hell we could get a lead on him, but I don't know how—unless some other guest at the restaurant can help. Not very hopeful.

"All this depends, of course, on our guess that Waggerson444 on Meet.com was Lander. And we do think that, don't we?"

"Hard to say," Bautista replied. "His self-description doesn't match what you're telling me about him. Lander's a lawyer, I assume with an LLB or a JD. Waggerson's a 'private investor' with an MBA. Lander's married; Waggerson's divorced. Is the age right? The height? Eye color? Hair color?"

"Let's check the print I just made of Lander's picture," Reuben said. Together they looked it over.

"Yes, those things seem right. Maybe a little fudging with the age. I think Lander's older than forty-five. But not by too much," he said.

"Waggerson and Lander could still be the same. Nobody reading his profile would know if he changed some of the details," Luis said.

"Luis, how can we prove that one way or another? For my own peace of mind, I need to know whether my partner is a cold-blooded murderer."

"As I told you before, Meet.com, and all its software, is located in Bermuda. The NYPD or the DA would have to serve process there to get the background information on Wagger-son444. And I don't even know if that's possible."

"Damn. It would probably take weeks to go that route. But without it, I don't think you can just barge in on Lander and say, 'Hands up! You're under arrest!'"

"That's for certain. I'm not about to tangle with a big New York legal honcho without a surer case than we've got."

"Even if we prove he was at the restaurant that night with Marina, I suppose he could always say he was the family lawyer and he was talking some legal business over with her—"

"And with no idea what happened after they left Quatorze Bis."

"I need another drink. How about you?"

"Okay."

Reuben went to prepare the drinks, and also to apologize to Francesca and Cynthia for deserting them. "Press of business," he told them.

"What do we do now?" Reuben asked when he returned. "I don't see how we advance the cause, beyond getting the restaurant people to identify Lander."

"Yes, that's the first priority—which I told you I'll do tomorrow. But, Reuben, I'm surprised at you. With your new interest in electronics, there are a lot of ways to trace a perp. There are twenty-first century methods."

"Please, Luis. I hate that twenty-first century stuff. All our damn politicians talk about twenty-first century 'problems' or twenty-first century 'solutions.' Now you have twenty-first century 'methods.'"

"Well at least I didn't call them terrorist methods," Luis retorted.

"Sorry for the outburst. Go ahead—what are the solutions you refer to?"

"Start with this, Reuben," Luis said, taking up his friend's pad and pencil.

"The first one's easy. Taking the print you just made for me of Lander's photo to Quatorze.

"Then, second, Lander, or whoever, had car keys in his hand when he left the restaurant. If the car was rented, we should be able to trace that."

"I doubt that's necessary. Eskill drives a brand-new Porsche, of which he's very proud. He commutes to the office you know. With his car."

"Where does he live?"

"Greenwich, Connecticut."

"Really? Greenwich not 'Boston'? Good. That means there's a good chance he has an E-ZPass to pay the Triborough Bridge tolls. If Lander had one, the Metropolitan Transportation Authority will have an exact record of when he took the bridge to go home to Greenwich, if that's what he did that night. So that's the second route to pursue." Bautista wrote down *E-ZPass*.

"Then there's the computer in Lander's office," he continued. "Again you may remember that all Waggerson444's messages were sent during the daytime, usually first thing in the morning, I assume when he got to work. So he was diddling her from his office. Not from a laptop or whatever he's got at home."

"That sounds right. He was probably afraid his wife would find him out if he arranged his trysts at home, under her prying nose."

"That was a pretty dangerous game, though," Luis said. "What if somebody went snooping on his office computer, or what if his secretary did?"

"He could guard against that," Reuben said. "There's a security system, and a password is required to open any office computer," Reuben said. "And his secretary couldn't get in to his PC unless he gave her his password."

"Who knows the password?"

"Just the person who uses the computer."

"No one else? What if one of your eminent lawyers drops dead, does that mean no one can get into his PC?"

"Oh, I forgot. There's a master list," Reuben answered. "The only copy is locked up in the office of the Executive Partner."

"Can you find out Lander's password from your Executive Partner?"

"That would be very tricky. Why do you ask?"

"If you can get the password that's needed to open Lander's computer and if I get a search warrant for his office PC, we should be able to find out if he ever visited Meet.com. We may not be able to get into his Meet.com file without his password for it—same problem we had with Marina's file—but at least we can find out if he ever visited the site."

Luis wrote down *Lander's office PC?*

"Is there more?" Reuben asked.

"Yeah. His cell phone. He talked to Marina/Hallie on it. Unless he's destroyed it, that phone should have a record of his calls to—or from—her. And, even if he's gotten rid of it, we can get the call information from the provider."

Cell phone was added to the list.

"We might just check his credit card records, too. You have to pay a fee to use Meet.com and you do that with a credit card."

Luis put down *credit cards*.

"Amazing," Reuben said. "It looks like you can build an electronic fence to trap someone pretty easily."

"Well put," Luis said. "That's exactly what we want—an electronic fence around our murderer, whether it's Lander or one of our other candidates."

"Right now I think we'd better get going or we'll be late for our reservation at Blue Hill."

"Just let me add two more items: One, to check John Sommers's alibi and, two, to pin down where Darcy Watson was that night." He noted these down.

"All right, let's go. What's Blue Hill?"

"A first-rate restaurant, where everything comes straight from the owner's farm. We've wanted to take you there for a long time."

"I'm ready."

"We can continue to talk there," Reuben said. "It's small and quiet. We can converse in riddles, in case there's a *Page Six* spy nearby."

Nineteen

BLUE HILL

Before they left to go downtown to the restaurant, both Reuben and Luis told their wives about their suspicions concerning Eskill Lander. Francesca took the news calmly, not knowing the man and only glad—or hoping—that her husband's open case would soon be closed. Cynthia, on the other hand, was incredulous.

"I'm shocked," she said.

"No more than I," Reuben replied.

"It really looks bad for him?"

"It's too early to tell for sure. There are other possibilities Luis is still looking at," Reuben said, not very convincingly.

Both men worried that they would probably be talking about the case over dinner, apologized for this, and cautioned Francesca and Cynthia not to speak Lander's name aloud. He was to be known simply as "Mr. X." And the mysterious lunch guest would be "Mr. Y."

They were seated at a table in the back of Blue Hill, amply spaced away from other diners.

"I don't know about any of you, but I need another drink," Reuben declared. All agreed to join him except Francesca.

"I have to keep my wits about me to confront the you-know-whos when I get home."

"If the truth be known, you probably need a drink more than any of us," Reuben said.

Francesca laughed. "I would love to, but wine with dinner will be plenty for me. Mama-dos—that's what my mother calls me—has to be careful."

"And not papa-dos?" Cynthia asked.

"I can handle it," Luis replied.

The foursome tried bravely to make small talk (mostly about the twins) but the conversation turned to the murder as soon as they had ordered their meals—New York State guinea hen for Francesca and Reuben, and poached Hudson Valley duck for Cynthia and Luis. Reuben also selected a 2003 Aalto Ribera del Duero as their wine.

"Luis," Reuben began. "You wrote down a whole list of things you wanted to investigate. Can I ask just how you propose to go about it? The picture of Mr. X and the staff at Quatorze is easy. That's the first."

"Then there's his E-ZPass," Luis continued. "Assuming Mr. X has an E-ZPass, and it's in his name, I can find out from the MTA when he used it, no problem. Then there's the PC in his office. I can get a search warrant."

"Are you sure about that?"

"Yes. Absolutely. Just have to clear it with my higher-ups and then go before a judge and show, as our manual says, quote, a reasonable belief that evidence of a crime will be found, unquote. Same with his cell phone. I can get a search warrant for that, too.

"There are only two little hitches," he went on. "First, Reuben, you must get the password to open his PC from your Executive Partner. You say you can do that?"

"I hope so."

"The second problem is: I don't want to tip this guy off to what's going on."

"How can you avoid it?" Reuben asked.

"You don't have to tell the person named in a search warrant about it. You just go to the premises listed—if the guy's there, okay, but if he's not, you don't have to run around and find him.

"So here's my proposal," he continued. "You can serve a search warrant in New York anytime between six am and nine pm. So if I came to your offices around, say, seven pm on Monday and you are there to show me Mr. X's personal office . . ."

"Oh my," Reuben said. "I'm not very strong on the law of search warrants, but are you sure about what you're saying?"

"Yes. Remember, all I want to do is to find out if Mr. X ever tried to reach Meet.com. Just that one thing. So I'm not interested in carrying off the PC, or the hard drive, or anything like that. So you show me his office, I find out the info I want and leave—probably in less than ten minutes. And it's all copacetic, done under the protection of a search warrant."

"It's none of my business, but my guess is you may not find anything," Cynthia interjected.

"You could be right," Luis said. "But we have to start somewhere."

"What if he's erased the evidence? I erase hot stuff on our computer all the time. Like my love letters emailed to the Police Commissioner and the mayor," Francesca said.

"Very funny, dear. There are about two dozen ways of finding out if someone has gone to a website and most people don't know that. I don't even know all the ways myself."

Reuben sighed. "Well, Luis, I don't like your scheme very much, prowling around my law firm, but I guess it's necessary."

"Good. I'll get a search warrant from Criminal Court as soon as I can get clearance Monday and we can do the search at seven pm Monday night."

"You, know, gentlemen, I haven't heard a word about Mr. Y," Cynthia said.

"That's because we don't know a damned thing about him," Reuben grumped. "Just that he was older, like old enough to be Marina's father."

Each of the men had a touch of wine remaining in their glasses, so they raised a toast.

"Now, let's have dessert. The chocolate bread pudding I saw go by looks delicious—wonderful and delicious," Reuben said. "And let's talk about something else."

"Now you say it," his wife cracked.

"Just one other thing before we switch the subject. You had written down to investigate his credit card records. What about that?" Reuben asked.

"That's a tricky one. It's not clear when you subpoena credit card records if you have to notify the cardholder before you turn over information. We don't want that to happen. It's too bad Mr. X isn't a Muslim, or a terrorist."

"What do you mean by that?" Reuben asked.

"The FBI and Homeland Security, and probably ten other Federal agencies, snoop on people with Muslim names all the time. Just say 'terrorist' and all constraints are off."

"Very attractive," Cynthia said.

"I didn't make the law, Cynthia. I'm just telling you the facts."

"Let's eat our dessert," Francesca said.

They did, amid some further speculation about what the twins might be up to at the late hour.

"I just hope the sitter hasn't been driven crazy by the two of them," Francesca said.

Realizing how late it was getting, Reuben paid the bill and they left the restaurant.

"Call me after your visit to Quatorze," Reuben said. "And try to get some rest."

Twenty

A NEW DIRECTION

"How did you sleep?" Cynthia asked her husband at breakfast Sunday morning.

"Very well," he replied. "I dreamed of flocks of New York State guinea hens."

"Well I didn't. I was kept awake by a truly horrible thought. Made worse because it seemed so ridiculous."

"Tell me."

"It was just this: I remembered what you told me about your 'Mr. Y'—Marina's lunch companion. Didn't you say that the restaurant people said he was old enough to be her father?"

"Yes."

"My ridiculous thought was that maybe it *was* her father. Maybe it was Dan. Which puts him in New York the day of the murder."

"Good God, Cynthia. That can't be."

"Think about it. Isn't it possible he had a major confrontation with her over his romance with Darcy Watson? We know, or at least we think, she disapproved. And may even have been jealous. Wouldn't be the first time an offspring resents a stepparent or potential stepparent. Just like Facini and Dan."

Reuben finished the cup of coffee he was drinking, poured himself another cup, and told Cynthia he was going to his study "to figure this one out."

"You certainly have made my Sunday," he told his wife.

Seated in the comfortable chair in his study with the door closed, Reuben considered Cynthia's theory. Yes, it was possible: Dan had a bitter argument with his daughter about Darcy Watson, was unable to bring her disapproval to an end, and then killed her. Unlikely, but the ways of true love are strange, as he well knew from a lifetime of observation. But how could he prove or disprove this bizarre conclusion about his old friend? And keep the police out of it until there was proof of guilt or at least a reasonable suspicion?

Reuben knew that Luis planned to return to Quatorze Bis with the picture of Lander. Couldn't he do the same with one of Dan? If Dan Courtland really was the mysterious lunchtime stranger, the boys at Quatorze should be able to identify him. But how could he get a picture? Even though Dan was camera-shy, the newspapers would have a photo, but Reuben saw no way of getting to any of his journalist friends to help him out on a Sunday. Then he remembered the professorship Dan had given to Jerry Falwell's Liberty University; surely there would have been a picture taken at that time. With a certain amount of fiddling, he reached the university's website and, with still more fiddling, discovered a group picture showing several people, including a smiling Dan Courtland standing next to the Reverend Falwell. He printed it out and immediately called Luis at home.

"Good, I'm glad I caught you before you went to Quatorze. I have another picture to add to your rogues' gallery," Reuben said. He told him of Cynthia's theory and his success at locating a photo of Courtland.

"I'll come over and collect it before lunch," Luis said.

Still mulling over the situation, Reuben decided if Dan's photo produced results, he would go to Indianapolis to confront him. He felt he would owe Dan a chance to explain himself.

Reuben ended his seclusion and briefed Cynthia on what he had done.

"I think your idea of going to Indianapolis is a good one," she told him. "You owe him a private confrontation on his whereabouts that Friday."

"I'm glad you don't think it's madness on my part."

Luis collected the new picture just before noon and returned two hours later.

"Well?" Reuben asked anxiously.

"Mixed result," Bautista said. "Gary, the maître d', and Jerrod were confident in identifying Lander. The other waiter, Matt, was less sure. But the majority vote certainly was that the man with Marina at dinner was Lander."

"Not exactly beyond a reasonable doubt, is it?" Reuben asked.

"I'll concede you that. But I'm satisfied."

"Now, to the more immediate question—was Courtland the first mysterious stranger or not?"

"A split verdict again. Jerrod, the waiter, believed that Marina's companion was the guy in the picture, but Gary was less sure."

"Damn."

"Maybe in a lineup, if it comes to that, Gary would change his mind."

"A lineup? That would please Dan greatly. He's big on law and order, but I'm not sure his sympathies extend that far. However, there's enough reason to think Courtland might be involved and should be questioned. I propose going to Indianapolis tomorrow to quiz him personally."

"Isn't that a job for the police?"

"Normally, I'd say yes. But I think he's as likely to level with me as anyone. And besides, no policeman could get to Indianapolis any faster than I can."

"What about our little excursion involving Lander's PC? We'd set that up for tomorrow, remember."

"It will have to wait until Tuesday, I guess," Reuben said.

"Okay, if we have to delay, we have to delay. But can we do it at the same time—seven o'clock?"

"No, that won't work. The Chase & Ward semiannual firm meeting is Tuesday at five o'clock. I'll be at that."

"How long will that meeting last? Could we meet at eight?"

"That should be all right."

"Good luck tomorrow. Let's hope your visit obviates any need for a lineup for your friend Courtland."

"You mean because he can exonerate himself?"

"Or because he confesses to you."

Reuben felt he must make sure that Courtland would be in Indianapolis the next day. He hesitated to call him directly—he wanted to raise his questions face to face, and ran the risk of revealing or at least hinting at his purpose in a telephone call. What he needed to do was contact Grace Wrightson, Dan's longtime secretary, but he did not know her number. He had a bit of luck in this, getting her home number from directory assistance in Indianapolis and then finding her at home.

"Sorry I'm a little out of breath," she said. "I just returned from a nice walk after church."

"Grace, I'm sorry to bother you at home, but I need to know if Dan will be in and available tomorrow. It turns out I have some legal papers he needs to sign, so I may send a messenger out if he's going to be there."

He realized his subterfuge was probably transparent—there were no "papers" and he would be the "messenger"—but he stuck with it.

If Ms. Wrightson saw through his ruse, she did not let on.

"Mr. Frost, what do you think? With the Indianapolis 500 about to take place?" she replied.

"Oh, of course. Does he have a car in the race?"

"Does a chicken have feathers? Yes indeed. With his long-time driver, Bruce Gemelli. So if you have papers to be signed, just have your man come here. If Mr. Courtland isn't in the office, it'll be easy enough to find him at the raceway."

Reuben made arrangements for his trip and return and then tried to concentrate on the Sunday *Times*. Without success.

Twenty-One

INDIANAPOLIS

If Cynthia had a sleepless night on Saturday, thinking about Dan Courtland, Reuben had one on Sunday, pondering the same subject. He rehearsed over and over in his mind how he could question and confront his old friend in the most tactful way possible.

Still drowsy, he rose early to get the 7:59 am American Airlines puddle-jumper flight to Indianapolis. Frost called Grace Wrightson from Indianapolis International Airport to announce his arrival. She was puzzled.

"You told me you were sending a messenger," she said. "Pretty high-class messenger, if you ask me."

"I apologize, Grace. I need to see Dan personally. Is he there?"

"He's out at the Speedway. You can reach him on his cell. Do you have the number?"

"Yes," Reuben said. He had not counted on having to chase his client down.

Dan answered immediately when Reuben called.

"What on earth are you doing here? Grace told me you were sending a messenger with some papers I have to sign—for what reason you've kept to yourself and not told me," he stormed. "So what is this all about?"

"I'd rather tell you in person."

"All right. Come on out here to the Speedway. Ask for Gasoline Alley. I'll be with my crew. Pick me up and we can go to the trailer I have nearby."

"I'll leave right now."

"Please do."

Reuben had no idea what to expect. He had heard Dan rhapsodize about car racing over the years, and had come to Indianapolis often to visit CDF, but he had never been to the Speedway. Nor had he ever had any desire to visit it. Car racing struck him as a noisy and immensely boring sport; he even felt silly telling his taxi driver to take him to something called "Gasoline Alley." The driver took him for an aficionado, an idea Reuben put to rest as gently as he could.

Gasoline Alley and the adjoining garages proved to be a sight the likes of which Reuben had never seen. An enormous complex filled with racing cars, each one attended by a crew of mechanics hovering over the engine and concentrating intensely. All Reuben could think of was a hospital operating room with a team of surgeons working on a patient. The most obvious difference was the high noise level coming from an astounding assortment of tools, hoses, pumps, drills, and heaven alone knew what else.

The strange new scene and the noise were disorienting, but Reuben was able to find Courtland's workspace and spotted Dan himself bent over a racing car like the mechanics. The two men shouted greetings at each other, and Dan led Frost to the exit and to his nearby trailer. Both were silent as they walked—Dan because of a premonition of bad news and Reuben reluctant to reveal the purpose of his visit until they were in quiet privacy.

The trailer was quite elaborate and spacious; it had been leased from a company that provided vehicles for stars' dressing rooms on movie locations.

Once settled in the ample sitting area, Reuben began speaking, slowly, gravely, and deliberately.

"This may be the most difficult conversation I've ever had with anyone," he told Dan. "It's certainly the most difficult one I've ever had with you. A friend and client for what, twenty-five years?"

"Something like that."

"I need an honest, straightforward answer to a simple question. Were you in New York City the day your daughter was killed—Friday, April twenty-seventh?"

Dan looked startled and then his eyes popped with obvious anger.

"I have an easy answer for that," he said, obviously suppressing his rage. "That answer is no."

"You weren't in New York on April twenty-seventh?" Frost repeated.

"For Christ's sake, Reuben, I said no, and I meant it. Are you doubting me?"

"I'm afraid I am. The New York police believe that you were in the City on that date and had lunch with your daughter, Marina, at a restaurant on the Upper East Side called Quatorze Bis." Reuben had stretched Luis's tentative conclusion into a certainty.

"Is this your idea of friendship, trying to catch an old friend in a lie?"

"Dan, I'm trying to protect you from more probing questions from the police. And questioning that could inevitably leak to your many friends in the press. So let's forget your prior answer and let me ask again—were you in New York City on the day your daughter was murdered?"

Dan sighed deeply and twisted his splayed fingers together.

"All right. Yes, I was in New York that Friday. And yes, I did have lunch with my daughter. It was the last time I saw her."

"Was that lunch the reason you came to New York?"

"Yes and no," Dan replied, now a bit calmer. "I flew to New York that day to go up to a country inn outside Highland Falls, upstate from New York City. I was meeting Darcy Watson there for the weekend. It's a place we'd been to several times—comfortable and private. And the nice rustic owners know nothing about Darcy's novels or my money.

"After we'd made our plans—Darcy and I—it occurred to me that I could have lunch with Marina and try, once more, to reconcile her to my romance, liaison, whatever you want to call it, with Darcy. Even though she had introduced us, Marina was very hostile to our relationship and I really wanted to talk her out of what I thought was an unreasonable, irrational, and jealous position.

"I failed. We had a very cool parting, which I have deeply regretted ever since that day."

"And after the lunch . . ."

"I picked up a rental car at the airport and drove to Highland Falls."

"Was Darcy with you?"

"As a matter of fact, no. Our plans got screwed up because she's having some work done on her house down in Pennsylvania. She got held up that day by having to meet with her contactor about the latest crisis, so it was agreed I'd go ahead to Highland Falls and she would follow by train Saturday morning."

"So you left New York sometime in the afternoon?" Reuben asked.

"Exactly."

"And your rustic proprietors can vouch for the fact that you were there Friday night?"

"Of course."

"One more sensitive question," Reuben said.

"That seems to be the only kind you're capable of asking," Courtland shot back.

"Why didn't you mention this last encounter with your daughter when we had dinner that night at the Four Seasons?"

"I'll tell you exactly why. First of all, I knew that it was totally irrelevant to any investigation of Marina's murder. And second of all, having been a suspect at the time of Gretchen's death—however misplaced that suspicion was—I didn't want to go through that again. And I knew that if I was placed anywhere near the vicinity of Marina's murder, eventually there'd be a shadow over me once again. I didn't need that."

"But now the shadow's there anyway. So best you tell me the name of the inn you were at and the names of the owners so the police can check your alibi."

"So you don't believe me?"

"Look, Dan, I may, but the NYPD will want to be sure. Please don't take offense. I'm only trying to help."

Dan gave him the information requested and then said, "Right now, I don't know whether to thank you or to throw you out."

"I understand. You don't need to throw me out. I have a plane back to New York in two hours. But just let me say I understand your dark thoughts. And I repeat: I'm trying to be of help."

The two men stood and Reuben was about to embrace Dan, but his old friend refused him.

"Don't hug me, Reuben. Just go away and let me be alone with those dark thoughts."

"Fair enough, Dan. Let's hope our next meeting will be a happier one."

"Good-bye, Reuben. Have a nice day."

"Assuming his alibi holds up, you can scratch Dan Courtland from our list," Reuben told Luis when he called the detective that evening. He gave him a full account of his day in Indianapolis and the information about Dan's trysting place in Highland Falls.

"I'll check it out first thing in the morning," Luis told him.

"You'll still need to check on Darcy Watson. Remember Cynthia found out she was at the Cygnus Club the night of the murder, and she apparently didn't leave the city to join Courtland until Saturday."

"If I'm lucky, I can get hold of her tomorrow, too. It should be one of her teaching days in New York."

"Keep me posted."

"Sure, and I'll see you tomorrow night in any event."

Twenty-Two

FIRM MEETING

"As you know, I'll be home a little late tonight," Reuben said to his wife at breakfast Tuesday morning. "I really don't want to go to the firm meeting, but I guess duty calls. Then there's the little matter of the detective work with Luis I told you about."

As for the firm meeting—he explained to his wife what she already knew—that as a retired partner he had no vote on any decisions that might be taken. But he noted that the firm's institutional memory was a short one and that occasionally he could help out with his knowledge of past events.

"I've kept the new partners from reinventing the wheel a couple of times," he explained. "And even if I know only about half of them, it's a chance to look them over. I keep hearing they're an outstanding crop, but I always like to see for myself."

"What are you going to say to Eskill Lander?" Cynthia asked.

"Nothing. Absolutely nothing."

"Just be careful. That's all I ask," Cynthia told him.

As soon as he reached the office, Reuben requested an appointment with Russell Townley. The reply from his secretary came back almost immediately—Mr. Townley would see him at once.

Reuben was sure Townley thought he had new information to impart; too bad the Executive Partner would be disappointed.

Just as he thought, the first words Townley spoke to him were: "What's new?"

"Nothing, I'm afraid, Russ. But I have a very delicate matter to bring up with you. I'm sure you're busy getting ready for tonight's meeting, so I'll be brief."

Townley looked startled, and his hands started their customary nervous fluttering over the pile of papers he had been working on when Reuben came in. He asked his predecessor what he was referring to.

"Russ, back when I was the Executive Partner, computers were issued to all the lawyers, including partners. It was decided then to have a password system, so that the content of each lawyer's PC would be private to him. Each person's password would be known only to him—and his or her secretary, if the partner chose—and to the Executive Partner, who would keep a master list of passwords. As far as I know, that system is still in place, is it not?"

"Absolutely," Townley said. "The master list is right here in my desk."

"I need to know one of those passwords—and it's not my own. I'm quite aware that this is a most unusual request, but I give you my word that I am doing this in the best interests of the firm."

"Can you be more specific, Reuben?"

"I really can't at this time. But if things go along as I think they will, I should be able to give you a full account of what is going on as early as tomorrow. Meanwhile, it is imperative that you not speak to anyone about this. And not a word about it at the firm meeting tonight. Is that agreed?"

"Reuben, I don't like this one bit. But I guess I have enough faith in your integrity—and your love of the firm—to go along with your request, on the condition that you promise to reveal everything to me just as soon as possible."

"Fair enough."

"Now, whose password do you want to know?"

"Eskill Lander's."

Townley's hands began to shake even more than usual.

"Good grief, Reuben, are you serious? What on earth can the problem be? Do you think Eskill is stealing from the estates he administers?"

"No, no, not that. But I'm not going to say anything more right now. I'd like to, Russ, but I just can't. And, at this point, it would be unfair to Eskill if I did so."

Townley sighed deeply as he pulled a ring of keys from his pocket, selected one, and opened his top desk drawer. He pulled out a folder and, with his hands still shaking, found it difficult to open. Once he had done so he looked through the pages inside and finally said, "Here it is. Are you ready?"

Reuben had taken out his pen and a sheet of paper he had put into his inside coat pocket for just this purpose.

"Eskill's password is RW35 . . . No, wait a minute. That's last month's." He riffled through more sheets and then said, "Now I have it. This is the current one."

Reuben hoped that Townley was right; it would not help the cause to be given an outdated password. But the Executive Partner's extreme nervousness caused him to have a scintilla of doubt that he might be getting the wrong information.

"The current password is XU21014Y."

Reuben wrote it down carefully and repeated it back for confirmation.

"Russ, I apologize again for putting you in this awkward situation. But all will, I hope, become clear very shortly. And please remember, no mention of this to anybody."

"I've given you my word on that," Townley replied a bit shortly.

"Thanks very much. I'll let you get back to your preparations for our powwow. I take it there aren't going to be any bolts from the blue?"

"I don't expect any. The only bolt I know of is the one you promise to let loose."

In recent years, the semiannual meetings of Chase & Ward had been held at the Evergreen Club, near the Flatiron district. It was not especially distinguished or exclusive, and its quarters were thought by some to resemble a Best Western motel, but it had the merit of admitting women members. Thus it was selected over the crustier (and misogynist) Odyssey Club, where meetings had been held for years before the firm elected its first female partners.

Originally, the meeting had been held over dinner, but now, with almost one hundred partners, that had become unwieldy. (Reuben nostalgically remembered that there had been sixteen partners when he joined the firm.) Now the members met in a meeting room set up auditorium style. There was no dinner, but drinks were served afterward. (Drinks had not been served beforehand for several years; at least since one particular partner's tongue was loosened by even one drink, to the detriment of efficiently disposing of the business at hand.)

Reuben arrived and sat off to the side, between two other retired colleagues, Kevin Rawley and Joel Patterson. He had glad-handed his way in, introducing himself to those that he did not know—many, but by no means all, from the recently opened offices in Los Angeles and London.

The firm's department heads, including Eskill Lander, took seats in the front facing the audience. Russell Townley, as the Executive Partner, went to the lectern and started the meeting promptly at five minutes after five.

Townley began with a brisk review of Chase & Ward's financial position, which he pronounced "as good as it has ever been." There was no surprise here, as the partners received weekly reports detailing bills sent out; bills paid and amounts still outstanding; and office expenses. Nonetheless, it was comforting to hear Townley's assessment. There was an almost visible glow of satisfaction within the room. Reuben noted the contented smiles of his fellow retirees; their retirement payments, geared to firm income, would be secure for at least another year.

Then the Executive Partner asked each of the department heads to report on "manpower needs." There were no surprises here, either, as the head of the corporate group said there was no immediate need for more partners. But he reviewed the prospects of three associates—two positively ("partnership material") and one negatively ("just not up to our standards"). The tax chief agreed that there was no present need, but said there was a "true star" coming up in the ranks.

Craig Haskins, the head of litigation, said more hands were needed—many more, in his view.

"We are nearing a crisis where we're simply going to have to turn down good business, and good business from some of our most loyal clients," Haskins told his colleagues. "And we've got the manpower to turn things around." He reviewed not one or three associates, but six, all of whom he described with encomiums ranging from "absolutely brilliant" to "truly outstanding." Other litigators chimed in to add their praise of the *papabile*. At times, it sounded like an election for new members of the Politburo.

The assessment by Haskins and his henchmen produced some knowing glances and eye rolling within the audience. The head of litigation was always predicting doom and utter collapse unless the litigation empire was expanded, and expanded with the luminous young candidates waiting to be tapped.

"We all look forward to making some selections in the fall," Townley said when his partner had finished. "However, I think it fair to say that you might do some editing of your army of worthies between now and then."

"That will be hard, sir, especially since we can use them all. We'll try, of course. You'll be hearing more from us."

"You can bet on that," Reuben's neighbor Rawley whispered to him.

Eskill Lander spoke next. Reuben paid strict attention and was pleased to note that Townley did not display any untoward emotion when introducing him.

"Our department is stable," Lander began. "We've added a dozen or so T & E clients in the past six months, most of them with substantial assets. But we still have the same old problem— our clients refuse to die. So you'll just have to bear with us as we wait to collect the estate fees we know are there and will be ours eventually."

"Kill! Kill!" came a cry from the audience, which provoked nervous laughter. Eskill looked startled. Too startled? Reuben wondered.

"I hear you," Eskill said. "But the last time I looked, the measure you suggest was still illegal. As to our present condition, we have enough T & E partners and associates to handle business. That could change, of course, if we have multiple deaths and there's lots of administrative work to be done, but for now we're all right."

"More than all right," Rawley muttered to Reuben. "What does he need all those people in T & E for?"

Reuben shrugged.

"Is the Courtland estate still the biggest client you have?" Townley asked.

"Yes, that's correct," Eskill replied. "Dan Courtland is very fond of our firm. I have the T & E business, and Hank Kramer handles the corporate affairs of Courtland Diversified Foods, inherited from Reuben Frost. Dan's loyalty is great. I think Hank will tell you that Dan prefers that his company deals with us, independent lawyers, rather than yes-men house lawyers. That translates right through to the bottom line."

Kramer, sitting elsewhere in the audience, nodded vigorously.

"As you all know," Eskill continued, "Dan Courtland's daughter was murdered here in the city at the end of last month. That's created something of a problem for us. He calls me every day to see what is happening, what's going on to solve the murder. He does the same to Russ, to Hank, and I'm sure to Reuben. He's got some fixation that we are detectives and can somehow get to the bottom of the mystery. I keep telling him that the problem's outside our expertise. He won't listen. And, of course, it's hard to make him understand this, given Reuben's reputation as an amateur detective. And I know Reuben's involved."

"Is that wise?" Craig Haskins asked. "If the murder remains unsolved, it sounds like our biggest client may blame us." As a litigator, he was jealous of the forays of a corporate lawyer, Reuben, into criminal law matters. Eskill had given him an occasion to needle—if not knife—Reuben.

"I feel the same way, Craig," Eskill said. "It's really better if *all* of us stay out of it." He looked straight at Reuben as he said this.

Reuben stood up, took a deep breath, and addressed his colleagues. He realized his response would have to include a touch of deception, but he had to explain himself.

"Gentlemen, ladies. I think you know me well enough to understand that the last thing in the world I would do is anything that would embarrass the firm or cast it in a bad light. I never have, and I never will. So let me try to explain. After his daughter's murder, Dan Courtland, one of my oldest clients and friends, asked me to get involved in solving the crime. Normally, there would be very little I could do. But as it happens, the police detective assigned to the Courtland case is a man I've known since Graham Donovan's murder years ago. So I have been talking with him. To that extent I'm 'involved.' That's what our client wanted, and that's what I've done. My role, if you can even call it that, is strictly passive and I don't think is likely to offend Dan in any way." *Even if the past actions of one of my partners may possibly do so*, Reuben thought but did not say.

"Maybe you can tell us what's happening, Reuben," Townley said.

"As far as I know, nothing concrete as yet. The police are exploring some leads, but my best information is that they haven't reached any conclusion."

"Well, keep your powder dry, my friend. And keep in mind the reservations that have been expressed here," Townley instructed him.

"I think you'd agree that I've never been anything but discreet and I expect I will continue to be so," Reuben said, before sitting down. His thoughts were confused. Had he been too disingenuous with his partners? On the other hand, he could not get up and say that Eskill Lander was the leading suspect in the case. Or that he was about to assist in breaking in to his computer. All things considered, he decided that his circumspection had been justified and correct.

"There's one other unpleasant subject I must bring up," Townley told the group. "That is the murder of our associate, Edward Joyner. As far as I know, there's been no break in that case, either. But let me reiterate again the two things I said in the memo I circulated to all of you after his death. First, that each of us should give all cooperation to the police. I realize that this Detective Muldoon that's been assigned to the case is a rather rough diamond, but please answer any questions he has frankly and truthfully. On the other hand, if there are any inquiries from the press, they are to come to me. *No one* is authorized to speak to *anyone* in the media about this. So far, I don't believe that's happened, so let's keep it that way. And on that happy note, unless there's other new business, I declare the meeting adjourned. Let's have a drink."

As he got up to leave, Joel Patterson turned to Reuben and muttered, "My God, what is this world coming to? Two murders that affect us, one way or another. But I guess that's what you have to expect in an anything-goes Blue State."

"I think it's a matter of coincidence, not a collapse of the social order," Reuben replied. Patterson was a rock-ribbed, die-hard conservative of long standing; Reuben, by contrast, was delighted to live in a Blue State and, in fact, hoped that it was bright, Cobalt Blue.

On the way to the room where drinks were served, several colleagues approached Reuben and said they disagreed with the notion that he shouldn't be involved in the Courtland case. He himself knew that he had to leave as soon as he decently could to meet Luis, so he had a very quick martini and left as unobtrusively as possible. In a way, he was relieved; he didn't want to be pressed by the others any further—or to have to dissemble at any greater length—about the situation. He especially did not relish confronting, and being polite to, Eskill Lander.

Twenty-Three

THE SEARCH

On his way to the rendezvous with Luis, Reuben was filled with apprehension; his whole attention was on the Courtland murder and the impending search of Eskill Lander's computer. His first fleeting thought was that it was a shame that Luis had found that American Express receipt at Quatorze. He soon came to the self-realization that this was a foolish and deeply flawed view. If Eskill was in fact guilty, he deserved to be apprehended and punished, whatever the consequences to Chase & Ward and to Reuben personally. Covering up was not an option. He was, after all, an officer of the court, bound by his oath as a lawyer to see that justice was done.

Nevertheless, Reuben remained troubled and nervous. He was sure Luis would act properly; the detective had called in midafternoon to say that he had obtained the necessary search warrant from a criminal court justice. And Reuben told him that he had found out the magic password.

"We're all set," Luis told him. "Everything's cool. There's no problem. I have the search warrant. So I'll see you at seven o'clock?"

"That's what we agreed to," Reuben told him, with notable

lack of enthusiasm. With the cocktail hour after the firm meeting taking place, he was sure Eskill would not be around. Still, Reuben was edgy about searching the man's computer in his absence, without prior notice. True, it would be done under color of a legitimate search warrant, but shouldn't Luis serve it in the customary way? By personal service to Eskill?

He finally convinced himself that he should defer to Luis and then began ruminating about Dan Courtland. If Eskill were found to be the murderer, and the facts of Reuben's participation in his exposure came to light, wouldn't his partners blame him if Dan pulled his legal business from the firm? He almost certainly would do so. Reuben could foresee being ostracized and shunned by the likes of Craig Haskins, ready to blame him as the messenger—or, more properly, the interloper—rather than the real culprit.

Reason again prevailed and Reuben saw his duty. Promptly at eight, the night receptionist rang to announce Luis's arrival. Reuben went to meet him.

"Can we talk privately for a few minutes?" Luis asked in a low voice the receptionist could not hear.

"Come down to my office," Reuben replied.

Once seated in the office, door closed, Luis related three "events" that had occurred that day. "It's been busy," he remarked.

The first event had been a call from his Suffolk County colleague who confirmed that John Sommers had been at the Almond Restaurant the night of the murder, leaving around nine o'clock.

"So he could have driven back to New York and been the killer," Reuben said.

"Not very likely. You remember he said he was at the restaurant with a martini and a book? Well, it was several martinis, and both the owner of the restaurant and the taxi driver who took him home told my colleague that he would not have been in any shape to drive back to the city, let alone to strangle Marina."

"What's next?"

"Courtland's alibi checks out. He was at that inn all evening and had dinner there."

"And Watson was not with him?"

"No. But that's item number three. I've just come from seeing her at that club of hers. She was indeed in town today and agreed, albeit reluctantly, to see me again. I questioned her about April twenty-seventh, and she admitted she had not been candid with me.

"'I figured anything about Dan and me—we were meeting up that weekend—could only confuse the murder investigation unnecessarily,' she told me, then apologized for what she had done.

"I continued to press her about her whereabouts that evening. 'Are you insinuating that I killed Marina?' she finally said. I didn't reply, and then she said 'There's one little fact you don't know, Detective. I don't drive. Never have. Never learned.' Then to emphasize the point, she took her passport out of her purse, explaining that she has to use it as her photo ID because she has no driver's license.

"She made a crack about 'hiring a taxi to dump the body,' but I got up, thanked her for her time, and left."

Reuben could barely suppress a smile as he thought of the surprise the novelist had caused.

"You realize what these events mean, don't you Reuben?" Luis continued.

"I'm not sure I do."

"Well, unless something turns up on that Facini kid—which

seems unlikely—our only remaining suspect is Eskill Lander. So let's get to his computer."

The two left Reuben's office and headed toward Eskill's.

"You have the, um, search warrant?" Reuben asked in a low voice as they went down the corridor.

"Of course. You want to read it?" He pulled it from his pocket and offered it to Reuben.

"No, no, I trust you," Reuben said, declining the proffer.

On the way, they encountered George Schoff, the head night stenographer.

"Mr. Frost, what are you doing here at this hour?" Schoff asked jovially. "Don't you know retired partners have to leave by five thirty?"

Reuben felt like saying "We're doing a bag job," but refrained from doing so.

"Just showing my friend Mr. Bautista around our beautiful offices," he said instead. *Mr.* Bautista, not *Detective* Bautista or *Officer* Bautista.

Schoff seemed satisfied and went on his way.

"Here we are," Reuben said as he and Luis reached the suite that included Eskill's office and those of Eskill's secretary, another partner, and that partner's secretary. All were absent.

Reuben tried the door of Eskill's private office. It was unlocked, as he expected. By long custom, Chase & Ward partners left their offices unlocked. The only one in recent memory who insisted on locking up every night, Christopher Pickard, was known jokingly as "Lock-Pick Pickard." Sensitive papers were, of course, supposed to be secured in files or desks, but otherwise, for no good reason other than tradition—the purpose of which no one could remember—there was an open-door policy as far as partners' offices were concerned.

Eskill's computer was on a stand next to his desk. Once turned on, the screen showed a box containing Eskill's name and asking for a password.

Luis sat down in the desk chair, Reuben standing behind him. "Okay, what's the magic word? *Open sesame*?" Luis asked.

Reuben pulled out the sheet showing the password, and passed it to the detective. "This is it," he said, again hoping that Townley had given it to him correctly.

Luis typed it in, and the home page opened.

"Great. So far, so good. Now wish me luck," Luis said. "Let's hope I get the info we want."

Reuben shared the detective's hope. As he watched, Luis double-clicked on Favorites. A long list of website addresses came up, from Find Law to Travelocity. All very business-oriented—and non-damaging references. Meet.com was not found among them.

"Don't worry, Reuben, that was just a stab in the dark," Bautista said as he typed *www.meet.com* into the address bar at the top of the screen. The Meet.com start page came up at once. Then, almost instantly, the user ID box automatically filled with the handle Waggerson444 and, seconds later, a row of asterisks appeared on the password line.

Immediately below these two entries was a square next to the legend "Remember my password on this computer." The square had been checked.

"Hey, Reuben! Look at this!" Luis said, gesturing at the screen and half rising from his chair in excitement. "This is more than we had any reason to hope for! I figured we could find out if Lander ever went to the Meet.com site, but I didn't expect we could go any further than that without his password for the site. And here it is! 'Remember my password on this computer.'"

Muy bueno! That little check mark just may have put Mr. Eskill Lander away."

After another double-click, the two were staring at Waggerson444's page at the date-matching service. There was no picture, but the same profile of Waggerson444 that they had already seen on Hallie Miller's page.

They then checked Waggerson444's emails as recorded in his Meet.com file. After checking the records he had brought with him, Luis grabbed Reuben's arm and said, "They match! The mirror image of the email correspondence in Hallie Miller's file. We've got him, Reuben!"

"Let's get out of here and go back to my office," Reuben said nervously.

"Just a second," Luis said. He was still looking at Eskill's email file at Meet.com. "Look at this, Reuben, he had correspondence with another girl besides Marina/Hallie, though it looks like it didn't go anywhere. But what a different story it would have been if his affair had been with her—BlondieforU."

"Enough," Reuben said. "Let's go."

Luis again sat down in the chair across from Reuben's desk.

"Okay, Reuben, let's talk business. As far as I'm concerned, we've got Lander. It's now just a question of closing the electronic fence around him."

"You're absolutely sure?"

"Look, he's Waggerson444. He made a date with Marina the night she was murdered. Add that to the Amex chit at Quatorze Bis and the identification of his picture at the restaurant, and we've almost got the fence closed.

"I'm coming back here with my IT man in the morning to

serve the search warrant. We'll take away Lander's computer and his cell phone and anything else of interest."

"The PC may not be his own, but the firm's."

Luis grinned. "Look, Reuben, I've been down this road before. The search warrant covers Chase & Ward as well as Lander personally."

"How about confidential material about his clients? What about the attorney-client privilege?"

"Keep it up and we'll make a criminal lawyer out of you yet," Luis said. "We're only interested in stuff relating to the murder of Marina/Hallie. And if we grab some evidence that's privileged, he can object to its introduction at his murder trial."

Reuben sighed. "I guess you have all the answers."

"Man, I understand you're upset, Lander being your partner and all, but the electronic fence will be all completed real soon, and you can put the whole mess behind you."

"Easy for you to say," Reuben said doubtfully.

"And maybe you'd better stay home tomorrow. Let us do some heavy lifting without you around."

"Gladly. And good luck."

Reuben had wanted to believe the contrary, but the results of Bautista's search convinced him that Eskill was guilty. But he still had one doubt: Eskill's motive. When he reached home, he sat and had a cocktail with Cynthia and reviewed the situation with her.

"Okay, we've established that Lander was having an affair with 'Hallie,' and one that seems to have been going well, at least from his point of view. They had met up that night just before flying away for the weekend. Why would he suddenly decide to kill her? It makes no sense."

"It makes sense if he were killing Marina rather than Hallie. As you've said, if Dan Courtland had any idea Eskill was carrying on with his daughter, he'd find a new lawyer."

"Absolutely. From Eskill's point of view, Marina had to be silenced before her father got any inkling of the affair. But how did he learn Hallie's true identity?"

"Wait a minute, dear, I have a theory. Remember that medical student you told me about, that showed up on the police's doorstep? Didn't he say that he had dated Hallie, but when things got serious, she revealed that she was really Marina—and did so at a dinner she'd requested they have? Couldn't she have done this again with Eskill?"

"There's one problem, Cynthia. Let's say she admitted she was Marina Courtland. Eskill would have been shocked, but all he had to do was walk away from the situation, he didn't have to kill her. She didn't know who he was, so she'd have no reason to mention him to her father. He could have just put an end to the affair and that would have been it."

"Maybe she *did* know who he was," Cynthia argued. "What about that stranger who approached Marina and Eskill at the restaurant? Didn't the waiter say he knew Eskill?"

"You're right."

"So he presumably said, 'Hello, Eskill,' or 'Hello, Eskill Lander,' or 'Hello, Mr. Lander.' Any one of the three would have been enough to tip Marina off that she wasn't dining with— what's his name?—Tom Waggerson.

"And just the mention of *Eskill*—how many Eskills do you or anyone else know, for heaven's sake?—or *Lander* may have given his identity away. After all, she did know who Eskill Lander is."

"So there was a mutual revelation at Quatorze that night?" Reuben said.

"That's what I think."

Reuben thought about this for a moment. "Cynthia, you may well be right. I think you've doped out the likely scenario."

"The fatal scenario, you mean."

"Yes."

Twenty-Four

CONFRONTATION

Tuesday morning there was an unusual tableau at One Metropolitan Plaza. Peter Leff, an information specialist from the NYPD Computer Crimes Squad, and Bautista presented themselves at Chase & Ward's main reception desk. Luis, after he and his companion had each shown their badges, explained that they had a search warrant and wished to see various properties on the premises (not mentioning Eskill Lander by name).

In accordance with instructions she had received on her first day on the job, the receptionist called the managing clerk's office, which handled the service of process of any kind involving the firm.

"Gentlemen, Mr. Rivera, our managing clerk, will be with you in a moment," she told them. "Why don't you take a seat?"

The two chose to remain standing. Carlos Rivera, the managing clerk, appeared and introduced himself. As they shook hands, he and Luis seemed to be appraising each other.

Luis explained the nature of the police mission and handed over the search warrant.

"As you can see," he explained, "we'd like to have a look for certain items in Mr. Eskill Lander's office."

"And what's the nature of this investigation?" Rivera asked.

"It's part of an ongoing attempt to find the murderer of a young woman named Marina Courtland. I suspect you've read about her in the papers."

Overhearing the conversation, the receptionist's eyes widened. Luis was sure that word about the search would be around the office within the hour.

"How does this concern Mr. Lander?"

"I'll explain that to him."

"Is Mr. Lander here?" Rivera asked the receptionist.

"Yes. I checked him in about half an hour ago."

"All right, let's go down to his office." Rivera appeared troubled; he did not look forward to being the bird dog that pointed out one of his senior employers to police-detective hunters.

Carlos Rivera knocked on Eskill's door and was told to enter. He did so, with the visiting officers behind him. Eskill was seated at his desk, reading what appeared to be a correspondence file. He did not get up when the trio came in.

"Mr. Lander," Rivera explained, "these gentlemen are officers from the NYPD. They have a search warrant, addressed to you and the firm." He handed over the document to Eskill.

"Searching for what, may I ask?" the lawyer snapped angrily.

"As the warrant states, we're looking for evidence relevant to the murder of Marina Courtland," Luis told him.

"What the hell! What in the name of Christ has that got to do with me?" Eskill now appeared even angrier, his voice rising, his speech punctuated with curse words.

Bautista ignored the question and told Lander the specifics of what was wanted. "We need the contents of your computer, any backup storage devices, your cell phone, any pager or Black-Berry or tablet, and any old-fashioned engagement book or calendar you keep."

Meanwhile, Peter Leff began disconnecting the central processing unit of Lander's computer.

Noticing this, Lander demanded to know what he was doing.

"Sir, I'm preparing to pack up your computer."

"You can't do that!"

"I believe we can, sir," Leff said in a calm voice. "It's covered by the search warrant, as Detective Bautista just told you."

"Is that true, Carlos?" Eskill asked.

"Yes, Mr. Lander, it is."

Eskill looked on helplessly as Leff continued to work on the computer.

"How am I supposed to practice law if you take away my computer?" Receiving no answer, he shouted out, "Wait just a minute—stop." He buzzed his secretary. "Get me Felston, right away." His secretary buzzed him back in seconds.

Leff was uncertain what to do. Bautista put out his hands in a quieting gesture. His colleague stopped work and waited.

"Jerry! Get down here! Half the New York City police force is conducting a raid on my office," Lander shouted into his phone. It sounded as if Felston was resisting. "I don't care who you're talking to. Get down here now, dammit!"

"Hold your horses, boys. I want to talk to my partner before you go any further," Eskill said.

The two policemen stopped in their tracks, willing to wait for Lander's partner to appear.

Bautista recognized Felston's name—a high-profile litigator specializing in antitrust cases. Though he suspected that Felston, a master of delay when it came to depositions and motions, was not necessarily a search warrant expert.

The group stood uneasily until Felston—a slightly obese, puffy, mean-faced man—appeared and surveyed the situation. Eskill gave his description of what was going on.

"Jerry, these *gentlemen* are about to ransack my office. They claim I'm a murderer and they're looking for evidence."

Felston looked the pair of policemen over, then examined the search warrant that his partner handed to him. He read it, looking severe, but did not betray either surprise or anger.

"Who is Bautista?" he asked, reading Luis's name in the document.

"I am, sir."

"Judge Wilkins issued this warrant on your say-so?" Felston asked.

"Yes, sir. On the basis of my affidavit. He signed the order yesterday."

"Why?"

"My affidavit, which is attached to the warrant, has the details. Basically, we're here because Mr. Lander is a suspect in a murder case."

"And who was the victim?"

"Marina Courtland."

"You mean Dan Courtland's daughter?"

"Yes, sir."

"Well, well. The police department's been under fire for not solving her murder—we all know that from the papers. So you've decided my partner is the perpetrator, the murderer?"

"We haven't decided anything, sir. But we have reason to believe Mr. Lander may have been involved. We're trying to find out if that's a justified conclusion or not."

"Justified by fishing through my files and records," Lander said.

"Not fishing, sir," Bautista said. "Just looking for some very specific information."

Felston read the terms of the search warrant again. "Can I ask what your theory is? Why you should be looking into the private records of a respectable lawyer?"

"I believe the warrant speaks for itself, sir. I'm not prepared to elaborate any further at this time."

Felston shook the warrant in his hand, then read Luis's accompanying affidavit.

"Eskill, they're legitimate, I'm afraid."

"For Christ's sake, can't you get an injunction or quash this warrant, or something? This is an outrage!" Eskill asked, pleading, still in a state of great agitation.

"Easier said than done, Eskill," Felston told him. "If it were a subpoena, we could move to quash it. A search warrant's different."

"What do you mean, it's different?" Eskill asked. "I'm just a stupid trust and estates lawyer. Enlighten me."

"It's different, Eskill, because your remedy for an improper search is to suppress evidence obtained in the search at a trial, if there ever should be one. It's not to prevent its collection under a properly issued warrant."

"What am I supposed to do, open all my files, my confidential records about clients, personal matters?"

"Mr. Lander," Luis said. "The warrant is very explicit. I'm not interested, at least at this point, in your files, or anything else. Just the items I mentioned earlier."

"Jerry, can they put me out of business this way?"

Felston shrugged and threw up his hands.

"What they want is very specific, Eskill. I don't think you've got a choice."

"Thank you," Eskill said bitterly. "Thank you very much." He got up and paced the floor.

"All right," he said finally. "Take the damn computer. But my cell phone isn't here."

"You mind emptying your pockets?" Luis asked gently.

"Now we're going to do a body search?" Eskill asked. "Want to look up my asshole?"

"Mr. Lander, just empty your pockets."

Eskill looked to his partner for support, but Felston remained silent.

Reluctantly, Eskill complied. His wallet, his pocket engagement book, bills in a money clip, loose change he threw down on the desk. And his cell phone.

Luis picked up the cell without comment, along with the pocket engagement calendar.

"Give me the Faraday," he commanded Leff. His colleague reached into his attaché case and produced a small black mesh bag. Luis carefully placed the cell phone in it. The calendar he put in a separate bag.

Felston, used to giant civil cases but not murder inquiries, asked what the Faraday was.

"It's a protective bag that deflects any calls or signals made to the phone," Leff explained.

"Jesus," Eskill said.

"How about backup storage devices for the computer?" Luis asked.

"I haven't the faintest idea," Eskill said.

"Who would know? Your secretary?"

"I suppose."

Luis ducked out and queried Eskill's secretary. It turned out there were no such devices on the computer.

"How about a BlackBerry? A pager?" Luis asked.

"Detective, I'm not a walking spaceship. My only electronic device you already have seized and put in that black bag. It's a simple cell phone—no fancy add-ons."

As he was talking, Luis noticed an engagement book on Eskill's desk. He picked it up and placed it in the bag with the pocket calendar as Eskill watched, angrily but helplessly.

"I think that's all," Luis said, once Leff had packed up the computer.

"Only one more thing," Luis added. "If there's anything you'd like to tell us, I'd be happy to listen. Alternatively, I think you should be prepared to come in for questioning. We'll be in touch."

"Gentlemen," Eskill said, "this whole thing is an outrage. I don't think the next time I see you will be when I 'come in for questioning' but when we're in court for a violation of my privacy and my civil liberties. And I can assure you that I'm not going to say anything about your slanderous and absurd insinuations without a lawyer present to protect me." He shot a very dirty look at Felston.

"Thank you, Mr. Lander," Bautista said. "I think that's all." Without handshakes or other farewells, he and Leff, carrying their booty, departed after leaving a receipt for the items taken away, in accordance with standards of due process.

Eskill slumped in his desk chair. "Thanks a lot, Jerry," he said to his partner, the preeminent litigator.

"I'm sorry, Eskill, but these fellows were operating by the book. Due process, you know." He was as upset as Eskill, but for different reasons. Was his partner a murderer? Impossible to believe.

"You know what I think?" Eskill said. "This is some of Reuben Frost's mischief. That senile old bastard was brought into the Courtland case, and now he's cooked up some psychotic theory that involves me."

"I don't know what to say," Felston told his partner.

Eskill was silent for a moment, then turned to Felston, still shaken from what had just transpired. "Jerry, who's the best criminal lawyer in town?"

Luis and Leff exited from One Metropolitan Plaza as quickly as possible.

"Pete, we're building the electronic fence," Luis said.

"What are you talking about?"

"I'll explain it back at headquarters."

Twenty-Five

THE ELECTRONIC FENCE

The day of the search, Reuben stayed away from the office as instructed. Shortly after noon, the phone rang. Reuben picked it up, expecting a call from Luis, and was surprised to find his caller an angry—almost incoherently angry—Eskill Lander. He had not been prepared for this.

After accusing Reuben of "making up an absurd and outrageous theory out of whole cloth" about the Courtland murder, Eskill made several rapid-fire threats. For the damage done to Chase & Ward's reputation, he would personally see that Reuben's retirement payments were terminated. For the damage to himself, he would sue for slander or "if you have put anything in writing," for libel.

"If the truth be known, I've never much liked you, Reuben," Eskill admitted. "You have a very superior attitude, you condescend, and you plunge into things you know absolutely nothing about, like crime investigations. You're a senile old meddler."

Furious, Eskill stopped just short of threatening Reuben with grievous bodily harm.

"Eskill, I don't think there's any point in continuing this conversation. Let's terminate it right now," Reuben told his partner, hanging up the phone. He found that his hand was shaking as he did so; it was not every day that one law partner made such threats to another.

Immediately, Eskill called back and repeated his vituperative outburst; again Reuben said that it was useless to talk further and hung up.

Then he remembered his promise to Russ Townley. Since events were moving rather rapidly, he felt that he should talk to Townley now, rather than later. He called the Executive Partner and asked if he could meet for drinks at the Gotham Club around five thirty. Brimming with curiosity, Townley accepted readily.

Meanwhile, the tentacles of the police investigation had reached out in a number of ways, all with the idea of completing the electronic fence.

First was the confirmation of the Meet.com material Luis had viewed the day before. Peter Leff accomplished this easily and made a record of the result.

Leff also examined the information on the confiscated cell phone. When he compared the data with Bautista, it was clear that Hallie Miller/Marina Courtland and Eskill Lander had communicated by cell phone, most recently the afternoon before Marina was killed. This was all confirmed by the calls received and calls placed as recorded on Eskill's instrument.

Then there was the matter of his pocket engagement book. Examining it produced a lucky break. On certain dates, there were entries marked as *H*, and on others, the entry *H-S*. He concluded that the *H* could stand for meetings with Hallie, and *S* for the times they'd had sex. Luis had encountered this before, with at least two egotistical lechers he had come across in his career, who kept track of their sexual exploits with coded signals in their calendars. There were no marks of *H* nor *S* before his visits to Hallie began nor any after her death. Eskill's desk engagement book, to which his secretary had access, bore none of these coded symbols.

While these analyses were proceeding, Reuben met with Russell Townley at the Gotham Club. They arrived at the same time and settled into a remote corner of the Club library. Reuben ordered a martini, of course, and Russ Townley, ever cautious, had a glass of sherry.

"You use this place often?" Townley asked.

"Almost every day," Reuben answered.

"Never had any desire to join a club," Townley said.

"I think you've missed something," Reuben said. "But to each his own."

"This is about Eskill Lander and the police, isn't it?" Townley said at once, showing his customary fluttery nervousness.

"Yes. How did you guess that?"

"There's a rumor all over the office, which I finally heard about an hour ago, that the police were searching his office this morning."

"Yes, I believe that's so."

"Why?"

"Russ, let me get right to the point," Reuben said. "In all likelihood, Eskill is about to be arrested for the murder of Marina Courtland."

"Reuben, you must be joking."

"I only wish that I was. It's a nightmare, and I fear it's going to be an even bigger one for the firm when the story breaks. You've got to be ready, and I want to help you."

"One thing at a time, Reuben. Let's start from the beginning. The only murder I've been focused on has been Edward

Joyner's. A total dead end, apparently. That dolt from the police, Muldoon, has interviewed everybody in sight and found not a clue."

"Well, before I get into the history, my advice about the Lander mess is the same as I gave you earlier about Joyner. A memo to all hands saying that only you talk to the press. No comment about the murder investigation when the press calls— other than the usual stuff about innocent until proven guilty— and whatever you want to say about Lander's standing as a lawyer, valued partner, et cetera, et cetera."

"History, Reuben. Chronology. Timeline. Whatever. Tell me what the hell's going on." Townley's hand trembled as he took a sip of his wine.

As they drank, Reuben ran through the sequence of events. Hallie's murder. The discovery that she was really Marina Courtland. The Meet.com connection and her liaisons with Waggerson444. The link of Waggerson444 to Eskill Lander.

"Why on earth would Eskill do such a thing?" Townley asked.

"Oh, come now, Russ. He was fooling around with Dan Courtland's daughter. If that ever got around to Courtland, Lander would lose his biggest T & E client and the firm one of its largest corporate accounts. And—can you doubt it?—Eskill would be thrown out on the street."

"I'm a little confused. The only way Dan Courtland would likely have found out about his daughter's affair was if she told him. And for that to do damage, she'd have to reveal his name. Do you really think he ever identified himself to her as Eskill Lander, rather than as 'Waggerson'?"

Reuben reviewed the theory he and Cynthia had come up with, that there had been a mutual revelation of identities the fatal night at Quatorze Bis.

"All right, suppose all you've said is true. How do we deal with Dan Courtland? Is there any chance we might keep his business?"

"What do you think? The clear answer is no."

"Another round, gentlemen?" the bar waiter interrupted. Both declined.

"When do you think this arrest will occur?" Townley asked.

"I can't predict the police's behavior. The detectives have to confer with the DA's office before they do anything. And I know they want to build the electronic fence as carefully as they can."

"The electronic fence?" Townley asked.

Reuben explained the concept as they finished their drinks.

Townley thanked Reuben for the heads-up as they got up to leave. "And this electronic fence thing is interesting. Just one word of advice, Reuben."

"Yes?"

"Don't you touch that fence. You could get a bad shock."

Twenty-Six

ARREST

After the search of Lander's office, it took the police another twenty-four hours to complete their investigation to Bautista's satisfaction. As he had told Reuben, he was not about to take on a lawyer of Eskill Lander's prominence without covering all bases.

Bautista also needed to confer with the District Attorney's office about the proper charges against Eskill. An Assistant District Attorney named Jonathan Perkins was assigned to the case. It was agreed that murder in the second degree—causing death with the intent to do so—was appropriate. This could lead to life in prison upon conviction.

As their investigation continued, beyond the computer and cell phone records, Luis and his colleagues discovered that Eskill indeed had an E-ZPass for his Porsche. The records showed that the pass was used on the night of Marina's murder to cross the Triborough Bridge at 10:14 pm, thus showing that he had had enough time to kill Marina after leaving Quatorze Bis and before heading home to Greenwich.

A check with American Express showed a charge on Eskill's platinum card for a three-month subscription to Meet.com, thus removing any real doubt that Waggerson444 was Eskill Lander.

Another check, with American Airlines, determined that Irene Lander had indeed been in California on the dates of her husband's various rendezvous with Marina Courtland, confirming the *H* entries in his diary. Further investigation showed her reservations at the Mark Hopkins in San Francisco on the pertinent dates.

By this time, Eskill had hired the best criminal lawyer he could find, Paul Illingsworth, a partner in the firm of Rudenstine, Fried & D'Arms, who had obtained acquittals in six murder cases, including two notorious ones that had made his name well known.

Luis brought Reuben up-to-date in a call Wednesday evening. He informed him of the second-degree murder charge and, after negotiations with Illingsworth, it was agreed that Lander would surrender Thursday morning for his arraignment.

"I should tell Courtland about this," Reuben said.

"Look, Reuben, what I've just told you about our arrest plans is strictly confidential. You shouldn't talk to Courtland or anyone else—including your partners—until the deed is done."

"Fair enough. Give me a call when I'm free to talk to him."

Luis called again the next morning. Eskill had been arraigned and released on a two-million-dollar bail, which his wife provided.

Reuben called Dan on his cell number and reached him at the Speedway. He went straight to the point.

"Dan, the NYPD made an arrest this morning of the man suspected of killing your daughter."

"Who was it, Reuben?" Dan shouted over the Gasoline Alley noise. "Who killed her?"

Reuben took a deep breath before he pronounced the name: Eskill Lander.

"I can't believe it," Dan said. "That goddam bastard." It was the first time Reuben had ever heard the upright Dan Courtland swear.

"He was my lawyer. My confidant. My friend. Why? Why, Reuben, why? Explain this to me!"

"I'll try as best I can. The police have the physical evidence that clearly points to Lander. And I've tried to connect the dots to figure out the answer to your question: Why?"

Reuben went on to explain how Eskill had made contact with a girl named Hallie Miller on an Internet dating service.

"He must have been mad," Dan said.

"Yes, quite possibly. But to go on, we learned from another young man who had met your daughter on the Internet that she had used the name Hallie Miller. Then when things got more serious between 'Hallie' and him, she revealed that she was really Marina Courtland. She told this fellow her reason was that she was leery of guys after her money, men who'd recognize her status as a billionaire's daughter. So she used a pseudonym."

"You're saying my daughter was a whore. Looking for men on the Internet."

"I grant you it wasn't the way we went about it, Dan. But it's what young people do nowadays. It's perfectly respectable, if not always entirely innocent."

"I wonder."

"Lander also used a fake name and fudged the online description of himself. He said his name was Waggerson and that he was a private investor from Boston. So Marina had no way of knowing she was dating her father's lawyer, though we think she may have discovered that fact just before she was killed."

"That evil, conniving son of a bitch."

"Now I have no proof of this, but I suspect that Marina confessed to her identity the night she was killed. They were planning to go away for the weekend starting that evening—a new and more serious twist in their relationship, which up to then had only been going on in the City."

"So once he knew that she was my daughter, he killed her?"

"That's my theory. He couldn't help but know your reputation for propriety and rectitude, and he most probably felt that you would pull your legal business if you found out about Marina's association with him."

"I must say, Reuben, even in my wildest thoughts—and I've had plenty of them these past weeks—I never suspected Eskill Lander. The most far-out theory I had was that Marina's half-brother, Gino, had killed her. I've got to absorb this news. Let me call you later."

That call, from Dan to Reuben, never came.

Twenty-Seven

CLEANING UP

As Reuben predicted, the tabloids the next morning had front-page headlines about Eskill's arrest:

HEIRESS'S KILLER NABBED

White Shoe Lawyer Arrested
for Courtland Murder

—*New York Post*

WALL STREET SHOCKER

Legal Big Charged in
Courtland Girl's Death

—*New York Daily News*

He dreaded going to the office, sure that he would be questioned on all sides. He was right.

When he reported to Russ Townley, the Executive Partner said he thought "a council of war is needed."

"We've got some decisions to make. Let me get Jerry Felston, from litigation; young Sherwin Taylor, from T & E; and Hank Kramer. After all, now that Hank's in charge of the CDF account, he's the one most likely to be affected by all this. That sound right to you? An ad hoc committee to deal with the biggest scandal in the history of the firm?"

"Yes. Sounds prudent. Maybe a female voice, though, in case we start playing blame-the-victim?"

"I suppose," Townley said in a not very convincing tone. "Grace?" He fluttered his hands upward.

He meant Grace Hartley, the most senior woman partner at the firm. A first-rate tax lawyer.

"Sure. Grace."

Felston, Kramer, Taylor, and Hartley, all of whom had heard the office rumors—and seen the morning headlines—came to Townley's office at once and took seats around his conference table. The atmosphere was, to say the least, grim and tense.

"I assume this means we lose the CDF account," Felston said.

"I think you can count on that," Reuben replied.

"I don't believe the hit to our bottom line should be our biggest concern," Hartley said. "What's our face to the public? That's more important. Do we need one of those crisis-control firms to help us?"

"That's ridiculous, Grace," Felston snapped. "We're grown-up men—people—and we can use our common sense to handle the situation."

"So, wise ones, let's begin. What's our obligation to Lander?" Townley asked. "He was a good citizen and partner for fifteen years, we must owe him something."

"We have to make certain that he has proper counsel," Felston said. "I'm sure he does—he asked me for a recommendation after the police visit to his office, and I told him to get Paul Illingsworth."

"Illingsworth—that self-important publicity hound," Townley said.

"Self-important, yes. But damned effective," Felston replied. "Anyway, I'll check to see if Eskill hired him."

"I understand his wife put up bail," Reuben said.

"Miracles can happen," Felston added.

"I hate to say it," Reuben interjected, "but I think, Russ, you have to call Irene Lander. To tell her how sorry we are and to ask if there's anything we can do for her."

"That woman. She doesn't need our sympathy or anything else. And I suspect if she'd been a warmer and sympathetic spouse, Eskill wouldn't be in the trouble he's in. You're right, though. I suppose I must call her. Another joyous task for the Executive Partner."

"And also, as I told you, you've got to make sure you're the only one who speaks to the media," Reuben said.

"Yes, I'll send around a memo about that," Townley said.

"These are all minor details, my friends," Kramer said. "The important question is what we do, what the partnership does, about Eskill."

"I think we've got two choices. Suspend him until there are further developments, or terminate his partnership right away," Felston said. "In other circumstances, I'd say 'innocent until proven guilty' and suspend him. But here the evidence seems so clear, I'd vote to throw him out. Wouldn't you agree, Reuben?"

"Reluctantly, yes. The evidence really is quite overwhelming."

The others agreed. Townley said he would call a special meeting of the firm for the next day, with a conference call arranged for the out-of-town partners.

"I'm also proposing, subject to everybody's agreement, that

you, Sherwin, get in touch with all Lander's clients," Townley added. "Tell them you are taking them over and try to answer the hundred questions they're likely to have."

"That's fine, Russ, but there may be cases where you should make the call," Felston said.

"I suppose. Sherwin and I can confer about that."

"I don't envy either of you that task. Very tricky," Kramer said. He changed to a mocking tone, "Hello, Mrs. Grady, I just wanted you to know that your trusted and revered lawyer, Eskill Lander, has been arrested on a murder charge. But don't worry, I'm here to look after everything."

Neither Townley nor Taylor appeared to appreciate the mockery but did not say anything. Townley changed the subject.

"Sherwin, I think you should take control of Eskill's files. Move them into your office and lock them up."

"In addition to that, I'd seal off his office," Reuben said.

"Good idea," Townley agreed as their meeting broke up.

By the next day, the press had learned of the attorney-client relationship between Eskill and his victim's father. They had also been told, presumably by an indiscreet source at the police department, that there was "a possible romantic involvement" between murderer and victim. Another field day:

FULL-SERVICE LAWYER?

Marina Courtland's Killer
Was Her Billionaire Father's Attorney—
And Just Possibly Her Lover

—*New York Post*

THIS IS HOW YOU GET BUSINESS?

Courtland Killer (and Maybe Lover) Was Lawyer for Girl's Father

—New York Daily News

"Just the kind of publicity Dan Courtland wants," Reuben remarked to Cynthia over breakfast.

"I wonder who tipped them off to the connection."

"It didn't take much digging. It's public knowledge that Chase & Ward represents CDF, and I think Dan himself has been mentioned as a client in stories a couple of times."

The efforts of the press to track down Dan Courtland failed. But he was almost as much a prisoner as Eskill, trapped in seclusion in his Indianapolis home with a security guard outside. He was beside himself for missing the final preparations for the Memorial Day race, but he couldn't bear the thought of coming face-to-face with the media types chasing him down.

His imprisonment did not prevent him from making his views known on the telephone, however. He managed to get through, without any help or encouragement either from Reuben or Luis, to Jonathan Perkins, the Assistant District Attorney in charge of the Lander case.

Dan expressed his outrage that Eskill had not been charged with first-degree murder. According to Luis, based on Perkins's account, the ADA had done his best to explain that such a charge was reserved for a list of special circumstances, such as the killing of a policeman or a corrections officer or a witness to another crime, a killing for hire or a killing in the course of another felony. He also told Dan that second-degree murder was the highest category of felony possible in the circumstances.

Then when asked if the death penalty was applicable and Perkins said no, Dan became "excessively abusive."

Then the *New York Times* had a break, scooping the tabloids. Ben Gilbert, the medical student who had dated Marina, contacted the paper's reporter on the case and said he had a theory, which he would disclose to the reporter if he were guaranteed anonymity. The reporter did so, feeling she had nothing to lose. If the theory made sense, it was worth the grant of anonymity. If it did not, she could simply forget the whole thing.

Gilbert told the reporter the same story he had earlier related to the police, jumping to the conclusion that Eskill Lander had dated "Hallie" and only found out the Courtland connection later. At which point, he killed her. Another press field day, with references and awful puns based on *double identity, double dealing, double blind date, double cross*, and, of course, *double play*.

Eskill Lander's office remained sealed for two weeks. He had made no attempt to come to Chase & Ward since his arraignment and, as far as anyone knew, had not been in touch with anyone at the firm—except when Townley called to notify him that his partnership was terminated.

Reuben concluded that the sealed office was an embarrassment and suggested to Russ Townley, after checking with Luis—who had no objection—that it be cleared out. Townley agreed, but asked Reuben to accompany Wayne Kidde, the office manager, when he emptied Eskill's quarters.

Once unsealed, the office yielded a few surprises. All Eskill's files had been removed and taken over by Sherwin Taylor, as Townley had directed. Inside, there was a clothes closet, which contained nothing except an old raincoat and an umbrella.

Eskill's worktable had no drawers, so the only spaces that needed clearing out were his desk drawers. They were locked, but Kidde had a master key, which he used to open the desk.

Kidde deferred to Reuben once the drawers were opened. There he found Lander's checkbook, a pile of receipts for some charitable contributions, monthly bank statements, and the related canceled checks.

The top drawer seemed even less interesting: a box of paper clips, a pack of rubber bands. Then there came a surprise: a folded-up piece of stationery which, when opened up, had a photograph attached with a clip showing Eskill and Marina sitting at an outdoor restaurant table, a nearly finished meal in front of them. The paper enclosing the photograph read: "Apropos of our conversation, here is a copy of the picture from last Friday. I have another copy, as I told you, which I hope I won't have to use." It was signed "Ed." As in Edward Joyner.

"Oh my God," Frost murmured to himself as he examined the note and the photo he clutched in his hand. He closed his eyes as he pieced together in his imagination what this discovery meant. It was clear: The hapless Chase & Ward associate Joyner had encountered Marina and Eskill eating al fresco at Quatorze and snapped their picture with the camera on his new phone. Then he'd blackmailed Eskill—presumably to support his quixotic and unrealistic bid for partnership or perhaps for money—with the incriminating photo, leading Eskill to commit a second murder.

"I'll let you take care of the books. I have no interest in them," Reuben said to the office manager, pointing to the shelves of legal tomes and bound volumes of past legal transactions lining the walls. He gingerly put the offending photo and note in his pocket, giving no clue to the others of their significance, and retreated to his own office as quickly as he could.

He called Luis at once.

"Can you come up to the house?" Reuben asked. "I don't mean for a friendly drink. I've got something you must see."

"Something really interesting, huh?"

"Don't doubt my word."

"I'm on my way."

Twenty-Eight

EPILOGUE

Luis was, of course, excited by what Reuben had found in Eskill's desk. The excitement was short-lived, however, because there were no other clues, no substantiating or conclusive evidence, linking Joyner's murder to Eskill. Muldoon, Luis's colleague assigned to the Joyner investigation, didn't have any helpful theories or ideas, either.

"I hate to tell you this, and this is just between you and me, but Muldoon is a MUPPET," Luis told Reuben.

"What on earth do you mean?"

"MUPPET—Most Useless Police Person Ever Trained."

"Oh, I see."

Nonetheless, Reuben and Luis were convinced of Eskill's guilt in the second murder, though they felt the motive was different from the first. This time, their suspicion was that Joyner had planned to blackmail Eskill by threatening to get the compromising picture into the hands of Irene Lander or Dan Courtland—or both.

"We've theorized about his fear of Courtland, and possible disgrace at the firm, but do we believe he really cared what his wife might think?" Luis asked Reuben. "You always told me she was something of a horror show."

"That's true, and my impression is that they were not very close. But Eskill would not want the facade of respectability and domestic harmony to be ripped apart for all to see."

"Murder's a pretty desperate way to preserve the peace," Luis countered.

"Yes, but he'd already done it once and, as far as he could tell, gotten away with it. And besides, you don't know Irene Lander. If you did, you might understand why homicide was the preferable alternative to confronting her."

"I guess I'd like to meet her," Luis said, laughing.

"No you wouldn't, believe me."

Despite the lack of clues, Luis discussed the blackmailing letter and photograph with Assistant District Attorney Perkins. At the time, Perkins was in negotiations with Eskill's attorney, Illingsworth, over a plea bargain; the proposal being discussed was a reduction in the felony charge from second-degree murder to first-degree manslaughter, in exchange for a plea of guilty.

Perkins broke off the plea bargain discussions after reviewing the Joyner letter and photograph, and remained adamant about a second-degree murder charge despite Illingsworth's strenuous arguments.

Ultimately, after a jury trial, Eskill was convicted of homicide in the second degree. His attorney made an attempt, aided by fancy psychiatric experts, to show that, when Eskill killed Marina, he had been "under the influence of extreme emotional disturbance." The jury did not buy this elaborate defense and Lander was sentenced to life imprisonment. He is now serving his sentence at Green Haven Correctional Facility in upstate New York, not too far from his home.

Sherwin Taylor, Eskill's successor as the head of the Chase & Ward trusts and estates department, was the only person from the firm known to have visited Eskill. Taylor said he felt it was his duty to check on his former boss and colleague at least once, which he did some three months after Eskill went to Green Haven.

Taylor's report back was a sad one. Eskill had gained considerable weight since being imprisoned, his Yale-crew physique gone. Apparently, his principal jail-time activity was playing solitaire. His contact with the outside world was minimal; entitled to have fifteen numbers on an approved telephone list, he had not bothered to list even one.

"He never mentioned Irene the whole time I was there. The only thing he would talk about was his regret at losing his partnership in Chase & Ward," Taylor reported. "'That was my whole world, Sherwin,' he told me."

At Taylor's suggestion, the firm makes a small monthly payment to Eskill's prison account to cover his minimum personal needs.

Irene Lander did not visit her husband in prison. Instead, she filed for divorce within a week after his conviction. She moved to San Francisco and was seen, on occasion, in the gossip pages on the arm of a glamorous young man. His amazing handsomeness and her tightly pulled face formed a bizarre contrast.

"I wonder how much she paid for him?" Cynthia asked, after a picture of the two of them together was published.

*   *   *

Some weeks after Eskill's trial, Russ Townley received the following letter:

Dear Mr. Townley:

This is to advise you that I wish to terminate the legal services of Chase & Ward for myself and for my company, Courtland Diversified Foods, as of the first of next month. I would appreciate it if you would render me final bills, for me personally and for CDF, and arrange as quickly as possible for the appropriate attorneys at your office to communicate with Wallace Mills, Esq., at the firm of Mills and Walsh, 100 West Washington Street, Indianapolis, IN 46204 (317-558-4100).

Very truly yours,
Daniel S. Courtland

Townley found the coldness of this severance breathtaking: no preliminaries, no oral conversations, and no communication at all with Mike Kramer, the lawyer on the CDF account, or Sherwin Taylor, Lander's successor on Courtland's personal account. And, most surprising of all, not one word to Reuben Frost, the man's friend and counselor for twenty-five years.

When he broke the news to Reuben, Townley tried to be gentle. Reuben told him that was quite unnecessary.

"I usually escaped Dan's rude side," Reuben explained. "Not this time. I never heard one word from him after Lander's arrest."

"He might have thanked you for helping to bring Lander to justice."

"He might have, but he didn't. So be it. I'll survive and the firm will survive."

The firm did indeed survive. Coming at a time when the economy was in an upswing, the CDF business was easily replaced. And the trust and estates department soldiered on with one less partner and one less client.

Leisurely reading the morning *Times* one day in midsummer, Reuben came across a tiny item in the Arts section:

> In a statement issued today, Ray Greene, president of Gramercy House, announced that the firm would not be publishing Darcy Watson's new novel, *Carry Me Back*. Gramercy has been the publisher of Watson's previous six novels, which have sold in the aggregate an estimated three million copies. No reason was assigned for the publisher's decision, though Greene's statement said that Gramercy and the author had 'departed on the best of terms.'
>
> Neither Greene, nor Watson, nor Watson's longtime editor, John Sommers, could be reached for comment.

Another short *Times* item followed two weeks later, announcing the marriage of Darcy Watson and Dan Courtland by a justice of the peace in Philadelphia.

Nearly six months later, Reuben received a call from Gino Facini. At first, he did not realize who his caller was, but quickly remembered he was Marina Courtland's half-brother. Facini asked if he could come and see Frost, with no hint as to why he wished to do so. Reuben, now curious, of course acceded, and invited him to the townhouse, rather than the office.

"I kept that card you gave me the night you and your wife came to the performance at the Dockers," Facini explained to Frost. "Not that I've got anything more to tell you about my stepsister or her murder."

"I think that's all settled, thank goodness," Reuben said.

Facini then explained his purpose in contacting Frost. He had just turned thirty and had received the full amount remaining in the trust Dan Courtland had set up for him and Marina—a quite staggering thirty-five million dollars.

"I've been thinking about this ever since I received the money," he said. "I feel I have to memorialize Marina in some way. We weren't close, as I told you before, but I feel guilty receiving her share of the trust. So I want to dedicate one-third of that thirty-five million dollars to some good causes."

Reuben recalled that Gino, had Marina lived, would have received only one-third of the remaining trust corpus. It amused him that the young actor would now get two-thirds and give one-third away.

"What did you have in mind?" Reuben asked.

"A bunch of things. Marina went to Brown and majored in English, so I thought of endowing a professorship in English in her name at Brown."

"That sounds very sensible—and very generous," Reuben said.

"Then, I want to do something to memorialize my mother. I've done some poking around on the Internet and came across an outfit called the American Foundation for Suicide Prevention. Seems like a pretty solid group, I think. They do good things, like prevention research. I want to set up a fund in my mother's name—Gretchen Facini, not Gretchen Courtland, thank you—with the income to be used every year for research.

"The third thing I want to do I probably shouldn't tell you, you being my stepfather's lawyer and all."

Reuben explained that all ties had been cut between Dan Courtland and Frost, as well as between Courtland and Chase & Ward.

"Dan hasn't spoken to me in several months," Reuben said.

"I'm not surprised," Gino said. "But what I want to do is support something political—something that will drive that right-wing bastard crazy."

"That shouldn't be hard," Reuben said, smiling.

"I was thinking of a fund that would make contributions to politicians who favor gun control."

"That should do it," Reuben said, smiling again. "But why, may I ask, are you consulting me about these things?"

"Well, despite your ties to Dan, I found you and your wife simpatico that night we met. And I don't know any lawyers, so I thought maybe you could recommend somebody. But now that you tell me your firm's not Dan's lawyer anymore, maybe they could take me on as a client?"

"That's certainly a possibility. If you're serious, I'll look into it."

"I'm damn serious."

Gino Facini became a client of Chase & Ward, albeit not on the scale of Dan Courtland, his billionaire stepfather. A young and up-and-coming trust and estates partner—following in the initial footsteps of the young Eskill Lander—was assigned to his affairs. He supervised the three gifts Gino had outlined to Reuben and also drew up a proper will and established a not-for-profit theatre company for him. Gino seemed to enjoy the fact that his legal needs were being looked after by the firm his stepfather had first retained and then fired.

Cynthia Frost's seventy-third birthday was the next January. Reuben, as a practical joke, enrolled her in Meet.com (sans photograph) as TwinkleToes73. It seemed funny when he did it, but Cynthia was furious when she found out. She calmed down when she discovered that it was very easy to deregister from the site, although she did not do it until after she had received two hellos—from a thirty-two-year-old Pakistani in Karachi and an eighty-year-old retired dentist from Passaic, New Jersey.

"Reuben, if you ever do anything like this again, I swear I'll run off with the first person who approaches me on the Internet," she warned her husband.

"Don't worry, my dear. I'm through with Internet match-ups for good."

ABOUT THE AUTHOR

Haughton Murphy is the pseudonym of James Duffy, retired Wall Street lawyer and author of the Reuben Frost Mysteries. He lives in New York City.

THE REUBEN FROST MYSTERIES

FROM MYSTERIOUSPRESS.COM
AND OPEN ROAD MEDIA

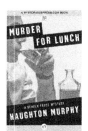
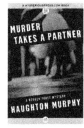
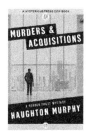

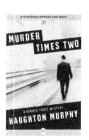

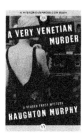
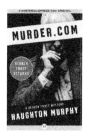

MYSTERIOUSPRESS.COM

THE MYSTERIOUS BOOKSHOP, founded in 1979, is located in Manhattan's Tribeca neighborhood. It is the oldest and largest mystery-specialty bookstore in America.

The shop stocks the finest selection of new mystery hardcovers, paperbacks, and periodicals. It also features a superb collection of signed modern first editions, rare and collectable works, and Sherlock Holmes titles. The bookshop issues a free monthly newsletter highlighting its book clubs, new releases, events, and recently acquired books.

58 Warren Street
info@mysteriousbookshop.com
(212) 587-1011
Monday through Saturday
11:00 a.m. to 7:00 p.m.

FIND OUT MORE AT:

www.mysteriousbookshop.com

FOLLOW US:

@TheMysterious and Facebook.com/MysteriousBookshop

MYSTERIOUSPRESS.COM

Otto Penzler, owner of the Mysterious Bookshop in Manhattan, founded the Mysterious Press in 1975. Penzler quickly became known for his outstanding selection of mystery, crime, and suspense books, both from his imprint and in his store. The imprint was devoted to printing the best books in these genres, using fine paper and top dust-jacket artists, as well as offering many limited, signed editions.

Now the Mysterious Press has gone digital, publishing ebooks through **MysteriousPress.com**.

MysteriousPress.com offers readers essential noir and suspense fiction, hard-boiled crime novels, and the latest thrillers from both debut authors and mystery masters. Discover classics and new voices, all from one legendary source.

FIND OUT MORE AT
WWW.MYSTERIOUSPRESS.COM

FOLLOW US:
@emysteries and Facebook.com/MysteriousPressCom

MysteriousPress.com is one of a select group of publishing partners of Open Road Integrated Media, Inc.

INTEGRATED MEDIA

Find a full list of our authors and
titles at www.openroadmedia.com

FOLLOW US
@OpenRoadMedia

CPSIA information can be obtained at www.ICGtesting.com
Printed in the USA
BVOW08s2120090616

451338BV00002B/4/P